Scone Cold
Revenge

Jan Fields

Annie's®

AnniesFiction.com

Books in the Chocolate Shoppe Mysteries series

Library of Congress-in-Publication Data
Scone Cold Revenge / by Jan Fields
p. cm.
I. Title
                    2017931901

AnniesFiction.com
(800) 282-6643
Chocolate Shoppe Mysteries™
Series Creator: Shari Lohner
Series Editors: Janice Tate, Ken Tate
Cover Illustrator: Bonnie Leick

10 11 12 13 14 | Printed in China | 9 8 7 6 5 4 3

Deep in the rough, long-neglected back garden of Belle Haven Mansion, Jillian Green stood frozen at the edge of the small clearing which held a pitted, lichen-spotted fountain. The trees that marked the beginning of the woods and wetlands on the property offered some shade from the summer sun, but they also seemed to trap the humidity and encourage the onslaught of buzzing insects. Jillian could feel a trickle of sweat crawl down between her shoulder blades under her light cotton blouse as she watched the woods intently. Her gaze remained locked on the shadowy tree line, her raised hand hovering halfway to her mouth, as if unsure whether she would need to stifle a scream or perhaps only a nervous giggle.

The thick brush of the woods thrashed, and Jillian flinched. A woman, her shirt soaked in blood, stumbled out of the patch of woods and stared around the clearing, her eyes wild. The woman couldn't have been more than twenty years old with short blonde hair that clung to her head in stiff, muddy mats. Her clothes were torn and scratches ran down each arm. She finally turned in Jillian's direction, her eyes wide with terror. "Help me! Someone, please help me!" The cries softened to choked sobs as the woman staggered farther into the clearing.

It was all Jillian could do not to run to the young woman's aid. She hadn't known it would be so hard to ignore the desperate screams and begging. Jillian took a step back because it was the only way she knew to keep herself from running forward instead.

The young woman stumbled another couple of feet, then fell to the rough ground, panting. She struggled to stand for a moment, then clawed at the dirt as she crawled toward the fountain. The thick brush rustled violently, and the young woman whimpered. A man burst into the clearing, carrying a long-handled ax. His face was ugly and twisted with rage.

The woman held up one bloody arm. But it was hard to tell if she was warding him off or reaching out to him. "Joey, don't! Please, baby, it's me. Don't do this."

Taking a step toward her, the man raised the ax high. Then he froze, staring down at the sobbing woman. The anger on his face melted away into confusion. He slowly lowered the ax. "Abby?"

Relief flooded the woman's face and she spoke in hiccuping gasps. "That's right. It's me, baby. You remember."

He looked around the clearing. Jillian saw his gaze sweep over her without notice, but she still shuddered. Broad-shouldered and blood-spattered, the young man was imposing, and Jillian felt her own fight-or-flight response trying to kick in.

"Put down the ax, Joey," the young woman coaxed. "Put it down, please."

His gaze turned to the ax in his hand. He seemed surprised to find it there and opened his fingers, letting the ax fall to the dirt beside him. The young woman sagged in relief.

Jillian's hand finished the trip up to her face, and she placed her fingers against her lips to keep from shouting to the young woman that she shouldn't trust Joey. She was certain this wasn't a time to relax.

"Joseph!" a gravelly woman's voice called out from just behind Jillian, making her jump. "What are you doing?"

The young man looked in Jillian's general direction again, his face still confused. "Ma?"

"Finish what you started," the rough voice commanded. "Do your duty."

"No," the young woman whimpered. "No, don't listen."

The young man's gaze flew back and forth for a moment, then he threw his hands into the air, dropped to his knees, and screamed.

The scream was still echoing around the clearing when another voice yelled, "Cut!"

The new shout made Jillian jump again, and she felt a wave of embarrassment at how caught up she'd gotten in the performance played out in front of her. They might be filming a ridiculous horror movie, but these young people were good at their jobs.

Savannah Cantrell, her best friend, stepped closer and echoed Jillian's thoughts. "That was amazing." As she spoke, Savannah pulled a hair elastic from the pocket of her knee-length shorts and used it to pull her thick brown hair into a ponytail. "I don't know if I'm overheated from being scared half to death by that scene or if it's just Georgia in the summer. I'm about to melt."

"I know what you mean." Jillian had been putting her own long red hair up every morning since the filming had commenced. She was in and out of the house a lot, mostly collecting dishes and mugs the crew left outside, and the hot, humid summer made her feel perpetually wilted like spinach for a Southern salad.

Annika Venn, the young actress and star of *Deadly Gothic*, scrambled up from the ground as one of the crew rushed over to mark the spot for continuity to ensure the actress came back to exactly the same place when they returned to the scene. "Is it time for lunch?" she asked brightly, looking directly at Jillian this time.

"Lunch is ready whenever you are."

Annika clapped her hands. "Fantastic. I'm starving." She trotted toward the group of men huddled around a viewscreen.

Jillian turned to her friend. "Can you stay for lunch? I can't thank you enough for coming over to help set up the breakfast room. This job has kept us busy all week."

When Jillian had taken the job to provide the film's craft services and have food available throughout the day for the cast and crew, she'd chosen the breakfast room as the best spot to set up the food tables because it had access to the back property through the row of French doors and was next to the kitchen. Since the kitchen, breakfast room, and family room were all one open-concept space, Jillian had emptied the family room and set up rented tables and chairs in there as well. The combined breakfast room and family room area was large and easy to clean up, which was a consideration with some of the mess the crew tracked in.

Jillian shuddered at all the bloody tracks she'd mopped from the beautiful hardwood floors. Since movie blood tended to have sugar in it, she had to wash away tracks immediately to avoid being overrun with ants. This had turned out to be a much bigger job than she'd ever expected when she'd signed the contract.

"I'm happy to help. I can stay for a while longer," Savannah said, "but I have an appointment this afternoon." Her smile turned mischievous. "It's at Greyson & Sons."

"Don't start," Jillian scolded. Unlike Jillian's family, Savannah mostly avoided matchmaking, but she couldn't resist teasing Jillian about Hunter Greyson. Hunter and Jillian had become friends, and maybe a very tiny bit more, since her move back to Moss Hollow, but Jillian didn't think it was quite worthy of all the teasing she got.

"I was just telling you that I would need to be leaving soon," Savannah said innocently. "I don't know what you're fussing about. I just want to fit in an introduction to Gloria Baxter."

"No fussing," Jillian said. "And I expect we can catch Gloria when she comes in for lunch." Gloria Baxter was the older actress with the gravelly voice, one of the leads in *Deadly Gothic*. Jillian knew that a part of Savannah's willingness to come over first thing to help prep for breakfast was because she was a huge Gloria Baxter fan, but Jillian certainly wasn't going to turn her friend away if she wanted to help out.

As they turned to head toward the house, Jillian heard Annika half-shouting at the director to pull his attention away from his clipboard. "Earth calling Chris! Can we break for lunch?"

Jillian paused and turned toward them to hear the answer.

The movie's director, Christopher Dark, looked up, his eyes nearly hidden as the bright Georgia summer sun had darkened his photochromic glasses. As he had every day since he arrived, the director wore all black: black T-shirt and black jeans with black boots and a slightly mangy-looking black leather vest decorated with fringe and fluffy black feathers. Jillian was surprised the man hadn't succumbed to heatstroke yet. "Yeah, that would be fine. Stay in costume though. We're going to pick back up here right after lunch." He raised his voice to a shout. "And someone check out Kane's makeup. The blood is showing up as two different colors on camera."

"That's my fault," the actor called back. "I cut myself on the ax, so some of that blood is real."

"How intelligent of you," Gloria Baxter growled in her rough voice. The actress wore her snow-white hair pinned up in a loose chignon that left wisps puffing out like dandelion fluff, a soft look that didn't seem to go with her personality at all. "Honestly, Christopher, couldn't you get a nice trained monkey for Kane's job?"

The director ignored her remark and pointed at Kane. "Get the bleeding stopped. We'll need to redo your makeup and shoot that scene again."

"I thought we were filming inside." Gloria stalked over to Christopher and glared at the director in disapproval. "You know I don't like being outside in the heat."

"This is Georgia," the director said. "There is nothing *but* heat here."

"It's worse in the middle of the day. We've talked about this."

"I know, Gloria, I know," the director said as he mopped his brow with a black bandanna. "There's always something with you, isn't there? But I need to get the scene with Joey, Abby, and Mother Penn nailed down today."

Gloria raised her chin and pulled herself stiffly upright, looking every bit the B-movie queen that she was. "It's in my contract. I will not be filming outside in the heat after lunch. You can adjust your schedule in whatever way you need." With that, she turned her back on the sputtering director and sailed past Jillian on her way to the mansion, growling orders to the harried assistant who trotted along beside her.

Behind her, Jillian heard Christopher muttering some things about the aging actress that definitely weren't complimentary.

"I think I'll wait until she calms down to ask for her autograph," Savannah whispered to Jillian.

"That might be wise."

Annika stretched and started for the house, soon catching up to Jillian and Savannah and falling into their slower pace to walk beside them. She gave Jillian an impish grin. "If Madame Diva keeps this up, we might turn this horror movie into a murder mystery, and I know who might be the killer." She giggled and nodded toward the clearly furious director. "All these delays are expensive, and Dark movies always come in under budget. It's one of his trademarks, along with lots of blood in every film. Gloria is killing the budget, and he's going to blow eventually."

"I hope not," Jillian said, giving the young actress a smile of her own. "It was hard enough talking my grandmother into letting y'all film at Belle Haven. Plus, she's been cranky ever since we had to have the sheriff's department run the protesters off the property. I think a murder might be more than she'll go for."

"Those 'Horror Movies Are Horrible' folks are nutty as pecan pie. I checked out their website after you told me about them. Seems like they blame horror movies for everything from poor college test scores to murder," Savannah said, shaking her head. "Plus, I'm fairly sure one of the protesters threw pecans at my car as I drove in."

"Could be. There's a tree at the end of the drive," Jillian said. "Though if Bertie catches them messing with her pecans, there really *might* be a murder." Jillian's grandmother, Bertie Harper, was an amazing baker who could elevate a pecan pie into an art form, which she insisted came from the fact that she only used Belle Haven pecans. In fact, winning blue ribbons at the county fair every year for her pies had set Bertie on the road to opening The Chocolate Shoppe Bakery.

Savannah chuckled at that. "It's not like we haven't lived through murder mysteries before."

"Oh? You've had a murder here? How delicious."

"Forget it," Jillian said to Annika, then pointed at her friend. "Don't start talking like that. I can barely keep Bertie calm as it is."

As Savannah chuckled, Annika stuffed her hands in the pockets of the dirty jeans she wore and rocked on her toes. "Well, we don't want your grandmother upset, or she'll stop feeding us. And that's my favorite part of this movie." With that, she took off at a trot toward the house.

Jillian looked one last time at the director. She definitely hoped

Annika's talk was just silly hyperbole. Savannah tapped her on the arm and pointed toward the house. "Lunch?"

"Right." Jillian continued the walk back to the house with Savannah. Though technically Bertie was in charge of the main meals with Jillian providing backup for the snack tables, her grandmother might need their help serving the hungry crew. Bertie Harper took feeding people very seriously whether it was catering an event such as the movie's craft services, or whipping up the fantastic baked goods that filled the displays of the bakery.

In theory, Bertie was getting ready to retire. That was, after all, why Jillian came home after living all those years in California. She was supposed to take over the reins of The Chocolate Shoppe. But her grandmother still gripped those reins as fiercely as an eighty-year-old woman possibly could, which Jillian didn't mind. She definitely couldn't compete with Bertie at baking, though she finally felt like she was pulling her share of the load at the bakery since she'd conquered everything from chocolate cake to cream puffs. And it had been weeks since she had last burned anything.

If she were honest about it, Jillian would have to admit that she never thought Bertie would just retire. At most, she expected her to take an extra day off now and then. Her grandmother's real motivation had been to give Jillian a positive reason to come home. Moving back to Moss Hollow felt like an admission of defeat when Jillian's life in California fell apart. But Jillian was beginning to see the return home as coming back to herself a little wiser and only slightly sadder.

Stepping through the French doors into the breakfast room, the cooler air was a welcome relief. Judging by Savannah's sigh beside her, Jillian could tell her friend felt the same way. The area around the long tables full of food was already bustling with crew. The crowd was made up mostly of young people who treated every meal like a celebration, laughing and talking with each other as they piled their plates high. Bertie beamed at them. Nothing cheered Jillian's grandmother like young people with big appetites.

Jillian walked back behind the tables and whispered to Bertie. "What can we do to help?"

Bertie's eyes turned toward the big clock that hung in the kitchen. "It's time to pull the scones out of the oven. This bunch sure loves them. I had to whip up a second batch." She shook her head in wonder. "I thought all the California types were afraid of bread."

"I can't imagine too many people can turn down your orange-chocolate scones," Jillian said.

"I'll grab them," Savannah said.

Jillian paused, noticing the empty kitchen and turned back to her grandmother. "Where's Aunt Cornelia?"

"Cornelia is upstairs communing with Possum," Bertie grumbled. "She told me that all the creative energy from the moviemaking is opening the channels to the spirit realm. Sometimes I honestly wonder if my sister needs to be medicated."

Jillian spoke slowly. "I admit thinking the cat is housing Uncle Raymond's ghost is a little odd." Bertie snorted. "But if she's upstairs chatting with Possum, she isn't badgering the director for a role in the movie. Every time she runs into the man, it turns into an audition."

Bertie mumbled something about being thankful for small favors, and then waved Jillian toward the kitchen to help Savannah with the scones. Her friend had already opened the oven door, and the warm scent of chocolate, with just a hint of orange behind it, filled the room. With her fingers protected by an oven mitt, Savannah lifted the scones off the pan and onto a cooling rack.

Jillian quickly grabbed a bald orange from the counter. Earlier in the morning she'd scraped off all the zest to put in the scones. Now she rolled the orange on the counter a few times; then she cut it in half and squeezed the orange juice into a bowl with confectioners' sugar and melted chocolate. She whipped the mixture with a whisk until the icing was smooth and glossy. She drizzled the icing over the scones, and then Savannah sprinkled them with a little reserved orange zest. The warm scones seemed to wake up the orange scent and made Jillian's mouth water.

Savannah sprinkled the last bit of zest with a dramatic flourish. "We make a great team! While you take them to the table, I'll clean up the icing dribbles."

As soon as the scones stopped dripping glaze, Jillian moved them to a plate and carried them to the table, squeezing them in between the basket of her aunt's fluffy biscuits and another basket of fruit-filled croissants. She took a step back and scanned the table, looking for anything that might be running out. Everything looked perfect.

"Should I help serve?" Jillian asked her grandmother.

Bertie shook her head. "I'm fine. Duck outside and look for coffee mugs. I'm still missing half a dozen from breakfast."

Jillian resisted the urge to remind Bertie that they wouldn't have that problem if they'd bought disposable coffee cups, but the expression on her grandmother's face nipped her urge to say "I told you so." She headed out to the garden with a tray and quickly found five mugs tucked into bushes or perched on rocks. She was still scouting for the sixth in the overgrown garden when she heard loud voices ahead near the old fountain. She walked to the point where the path turned toward the area.

Christopher Dark stood with his hands on his hips, glaring at Bibi Bleu, Gloria Baxter's personal assistant. Jillian noticed that one of the black feathers from his vest had migrated to his hair, which would have been funny if his tone wasn't so fierce. "You have to get the old lady under control. We can't keep bleeding money. If she keeps this up, she's going to kill the film, and I'm flatly not going to let that happen."

"I assure you, Miss Baxter is doing her best."

"That's not good news," the director said. "She shows up to shoots late, when she bothers to show up at all, and she forgets half her lines. She's already cost me too much on this production. If you don't do something about this, I will."

At that, he brushed past the assistant and stormed by Jillian without any sign of having seen her. On the other hand, Bibi Bleu clearly saw her, and the assistant's round face reddened. "I hope you won't repeat anything you heard here."

"I'm not a gossip." Jillian spotted the last mug perched on the edge of the fountain and pointed. "I'm just collecting coffee cups."

Bibi nodded and walked beside Jillian toward the house. "Gloria is just feeling the heat a little more than the rest of us. I don't know why Christopher can't understand that."

"It is a hot summer," Jillian said agreeably, not really wanting to get involved with the drama. Neither of them had much to say after that, and they walked quietly toward the mansion. Ahead, Jillian spotted something that made her smile, and she picked up her pace.

Her favorite actor in the production was just reaching the doors to the breakfast room. The tall man actually had to duck the doorway, even after removing his cowboy hat as he passed through the door. Leo Shone had done his first acting at the tail end of the Western movie craze. Back then he was cast as the mischievous towheaded boy who often popped up to admire the hero. Now he was a handsome, long-legged actor in his mid-seventies with silver hair and sunbaked skin. He also owned a ranch in Colorado that he loved to talk about when his attention wasn't focused elsewhere.

Jillian entered Belle Haven right behind him, watching as he headed directly toward Bertie the instant he came through the door. His long legs quickly carried him the short distance to the table.

Bertie's scowl brought a smile to Jillian's lips as she walked to the kitchen with an armload of mugs. Savannah raised her eyebrows quizzically at Jillian's grin. Jillian nodded toward the food table. The two friends gave up any pretense of working and leaned against the counter to watch the lanky actor's latest attempt to flirt with Bertie.

"You set a wonderful spread, Miz Harper," Leo said in his smooth Texas drawl as he lingered at the end of the table where Bertie stood with her arms crossed, eyeing him suspiciously. He had green eyes, craggy features, and a slow easy grin that made him hard not to like, though Bertie did seem to work hard at it.

"Thank you," Bertie said, her tone slightly sharp. "You best get a plate while there's still food left or you'll miss out entirely."

"The crew does put a fellow in mind of locusts," Leo said with a chuckle that Bertie didn't join. Jillian felt bad for him. He had been trying to charm her grandmother since the moment he'd shown up with the rest of the crew four days ago, but the harder he tried, the more determined she was to be annoyed by him.

Considering how pushy Bertie was about Jillian's love life, she didn't seem to be open to possibilities in her own. Still, Jillian wasn't convinced her grandmother was as impervious to Leo's charms as she pretended. Originally, when Jillian had lobbied to let the film crew use part of the house and grounds, Bertie had tentatively agreed, but insisted she never have to come in contact with them.

Then later, when The Chocolate Shoppe Bakery took on the catering job for the craft services table, Bertie had agreed to supply the food for three meals a day, but again she insisted Jillian would have to handle all the on-site serving and cleanup. "I'll be staying in the bakery," Bertie had grumbled. "Looking after my real customers. I don't need any of that Hollywood craziness in my life."

But then Bertie had met the handsome cowboy, and despite how many times she rebuffed his attempts to charm her, she certainly had found more and more excuses to be back at the house to help out during meals.

Reluctantly, Jillian turned her gaze from the unlikely romance and looked over the crew scattered around the room. Most were seated and eating enthusiastically. She noticed that Annika scattered bits of moss and dirt every time she moved, but it didn't seem to keep her from enjoying one of the blackberry-filled croissants Bertie had brought from the bakery.

Though nearly all of the actors, camera crew, and technicians were at the group of tables, Jillian noticed that Gloria Baxter wasn't among them. Considering how much the older woman had complained about the heat, Jillian expected her to be inside soaking up the air-conditioning and sipping iced sweet tea.

Apparently Savannah had noticed as well. "Do you think Gloria will be in soon? I have to run to that meeting with Hunter, and I really wanted to get her autograph." Since Savannah handled the bookkeeping for most of the small businesses in Moss Hollow, she was often on the run to one meeting or another, so it was a real reflection of her admiration for Gloria that she'd carved out so much time to be at Belle Haven.

"I expected her by now, actually." Jillian walked out over to the serving tables and touched Leo on the arm. "Did you see Gloria outside?"

He turned from piling his plate full of small sandwiches. "No. She was scrapping with Christopher a bit, but I figured she came in after that." He shook his head. "That woman would argue with mud in a jar."

"I saw Christopher," Jillian said. "Gloria wasn't with him—but Bibi was." As she scanned the room, she saw Bibi was missing as well, even though she must have come in right after Jillian.

"Gloria might have used a different door," Bertie said, "and gone right up to her room."

They were hosting several of the key crew members at the mansion including the four main actors, Gloria's assistant, and the director. The rest all drove in each morning from the Raindrop Motel out near the highway, braving the protesters at the end of the driveway, who all seemed to be early risers with loud voices.

At first, Bertie had resisted having any of those "Hollywood types" stay at her home, but the money they offered would go a long way toward finishing the improvements to the house and grounds, which would then make it easier for them to host events on the property. The bakery was doing well with the summer tourist boom, but Jillian was always aware of expenses. A big estate like Belle Haven was a lot to support with a small bakery, even if it was the best in the state.

With effort, Jillian dragged her attention back to the conversation. "Gloria probably did go to her room. She was suffering from the heat and may have wanted to lie down." Jillian turned to see her friend's disappointed face. Then she had a thought. "Savannah and I will take her up a glass of iced tea. She loves our sweet tea."

"Suit yourself," Bertie said, "but don't go giving her the idea we have room service here, or you'll be fetching and carrying stuff up and down the stairs all day long. That woman's a taker. I've seen her type before."

"I'll try not to look too eager to please." Jillian poured a glass of tea from the beverage table, and Savannah carried it as they walked through the living room and up the gently curving stairs to the second floor. Light poured down from the stained glass dome that topped the stairs above the third floor and cast bits of golden color on the stair rail.

Through some extremely careful budgeting and lots of help from friends, Belle Haven was slowly coming back to the beautiful home it had once been before tough times forced the family to let things go. There were still rooms that offered views of peeling wallpaper and questionable plumbing, but Jillian was proud of what they were accomplishing. She had begun to believe they might actually see the whole house restored to its antebellum splendor, something their flyers already promised.

Both Jillian and her aunt had bedrooms on the second floor, but they'd squeezed as many people as they could into the other second-floor rooms. Jillian had even given up her normal room and was presently camped out in what had been mostly a storage room, judging by the mismatched furniture she had to push to the walls to make room for a bed. At least she got to stay on the second floor. Poor Leo was exiled to a tiny bedroom carved out of the attic on the third floor. Technically, they could have put some of the film crew in the apartment that sat over the garage, since it was connected to the house by a long hall, but that apartment had its own outside access, and Jillian hadn't wanted strangers staying out there, even though making Leo stay on the spooky third floor made her feel guilty.

Jillian had been scared to death of that whole third floor as a kid because of the creepy portrait gallery and that single small bedroom. Someone at school had told her the original builder of the mansion, Captain Hoyt Belle, kept his wife locked up in that room after swamp fever had driven her mad. It was years before she realized the kid stole that idea from some movie, and the room was actually the last of the old servants' quarters. Still the small room made her so uneasy even now that she'd left it off the last time she'd given anyone a whole house tour.

Jillian sneaked a glance at her friend's excited face and hoped Gloria wouldn't snap at them. She suspected it would devastate Savannah if the actress treated her like she treated so many of the people on the set. They walked around the balcony to reach Gloria Baxter's room, and Jillian tapped on the door. She shifted from foot to foot as she waited for a reply. When none came, she looked at Savannah's disappointed expression again. She didn't want Savannah to leave without meeting Gloria.

"Maybe she's in the bathroom and didn't hear us knock." Jillian eased the door open. "Miss Baxter? We brought you some tea."

She looked around the room. The actress was almost military in her habits, and the room was impeccably well ordered. The rollaway bed she'd insisted upon so her assistant could be available twenty-four hours a day was folded up and tucked in beside the dresser. "Miss Baxter?" Jillian was about to give up when she noticed the bathroom door was cracked open. She turned back to Savannah. "She might be in there."

Savannah peered over Jillian's shoulder. "Can we wait until she comes out?"

"Maybe, but I wonder why she doesn't answer." The bathroom door was open, so the actress must have heard Jillian call. "Miss Baxter," she said loudly as she stepped into the bedroom. "We brought you some tea."

She listened intently but heard nothing from the bathroom. Jillian realized the room was probably empty, but she had a nagging tug of concern. Gloria had complained about the heat, and Jillian knew how many older people suffered heatstroke during the hot

Georgia summers. Could the actress be lying ill in the bathroom? Jillian crossed the room and tapped on the bathroom door frame.

"Should we be in here?" Savannah whispered.

"Miss Baxter?" Jillian called. As she stepped around the open door a sharp, metallic scent hit her nose. She knew that smell. It was blood!

On the snow-white tile floor, a huge black crow lay in a puddle of blood. In the light from the bathroom window, the crow's inky feathers shone with hints of blue and purple, and splatters of red.

"Oh, the poor thing," Savannah said as she joined Jillian in the bathroom doorway. "What do you think happened to it?"

Jillian forced her gaze away from the lifeless creature and toward the small bathroom window. "It's a big bird. I suppose it could have hit a window and broken through." But the bathroom window was whole and closed, as was the second bathroom door that led to Annika's room. The two actresses had to share a bathroom, which seemed to infuriate Gloria and amuse Annika.

Jillian tried to decide what to do about the dead bird. Should they even touch it? Didn't birds carry disease? She took a tentative step into the bathroom, careful to avoid the blood spatters.

She pulled down one of the towels from the towel bar and gently placed it over the body. Though she knew there was no way she could cause it pain, she still wrapped it gently and picked it up, wiping up most of the blood at the same time. She tucked the bloody part of the towel to the inside so no one would see it as she got rid of the dead bird.

"Are you sure it's dead?" Savannah asked. "I could take it to the vet. He's a client; I'm sure he would understand."

"It's too late, but we certainly need to get it out of here. I'll come back and clean up the mess. If I sacrifice more than one of Bertie's towels, she'll have my head." Jillian carried the bird out through the bedroom and into the hall, where she almost ran into her aunt. Cornelia was wearing one of her many floaty floral dresses and carrying a smoking bundle of sage, the earthy herb aroma wafting around her.

"What do you have there?" Cornelia asked, gesturing with the smoldering sage and sending the smoke up Jillian's nose, making her sneeze.

Savannah stepped up to answer while Jillian sneezed again. "A dead crow. It was in Gloria Baxter's bathroom."

Jillian gestured toward the herbs in Cornelia's hand, wishing she had a clean hand to press to her nose. "If Bertie sees you with that, she's going to flip. You know she hates that sort of thing."

"All these strangers in the house have disrupted the spiritual atmosphere," Cornelia said. "I'm bringing balance." She waved the stick again, releasing a fresh waft of smoke and provoking more sneezes. "Bless you," Cornelia said. "You know the Victorians believed sneezing was good for you. My grandmother always said it blew the dust off your brains."

Savannah laughed at that, but Jillian only stepped away from her aunt to get out of the path of the smoke. "I prefer my brain dusty." She nodded at the smoking herbs. "As long as none of our guests break out in hives from the smoke, I'm fine with it. But I'd still be careful. Bertie is already grumpy over strangers in the house, protesters practically on the lawn, and Leo Shone flirting shamelessly with her. She's not going to be any happier when I tell her there was a bloody bird carcass in one of our bathrooms."

"Bloody?" Cornelia echoed, stepping closer to the bird and nearly igniting the towel with the smoldering sage stick until Jillian jumped back.

Jillian checked the underside of the towel and saw a distinct smudge. Between the soot and the blood, she wondered if it would ever come clean.

"Why is it bloody? In fact, why is it dead?" Cornelia asked. "And what kind of bird is it?"

"It's a crow," Savannah volunteered.

"I don't know why it's dead." Jillian looked up from the sad bundle. "I thought maybe it had flown against a window. It's a large bird. If it was flying fast, I could imagine it breaking the glass, but the window in the bathroom was intact. I don't know how it got there."

Cornelia turned and swept into Gloria Baxter's room. "Then it must be one of the other windows. The bird might have made it from the bedroom to the bathroom before it died. I'll check."

"Aunt Cornelia," Jillian called. "Don't smoke up that room. You know how particular Miss Baxter is. Savannah and I can check."

"Actually I can't," Savannah said, her voice apologetic. "If you don't need me to run the bird to the vet, I have to leave. If I stay any longer, I'm not going to make my appointment at Greyson & Sons on time. I could call and postpone. I will if you need me to. Hunter would certainly understand since it's you."

Jillian thought that Savannah was overestimating Hunter's fondness for her, but she didn't comment on that and merely shook her head. "I can handle it. You should go on. Tell Hunter hello for me. Thanks for helping with everything, Savannah. I'm sure you'll get another chance at Gloria's autograph. They're scheduled to be here another two weeks."

"I hope so." Savannah gave one last sad look toward the bundle in Jillian's hands. Then with a little wave, she left.

Jillian walked into the actress's room to find that Cornelia had managed to push aside one of the window drapes without setting fire to it. "You should take that smoking thing outside."

"Nonsense," her aunt said. "I am certain that Miss Baxter will appreciate the spiritual cleansing when she finds out something died in here."

Jillian followed her aunt into the room. "I wasn't intending to tell her something died in here. I was kind of hoping to get everything cleaned before she came back."

Cornelia gave her a disapproving look. "You have to tell her. She really must be warned about the forces violent death stirs up."

"Forces?" Jillian shook her head before she could ask more questions. She was being pulled off track again.

Cornelia pointed toward the bundle in Jillian's hands. "Judging by the size of that, it's a raven. And everyone knows that ravens are messengers from the spiritual realm. The bird may be trying to communicate something."

Jillian sighed. "I think its communication days are over. How about we just check to see if the windows are intact and get out of here?"

Cornelia dropped the drape. "This one is fine." She pushed aside the curtain for the next window and it was intact as well. Both windows were closed tight to keep out the thick, hot summer air.

"That doesn't make sense," Jillian said. "The bedroom door was closed. And so was the door to Annika's bedroom. So how did the crow get in?"

"That is an interesting question." Cornelia looked at the wadded towel in Jillian's hands. "Are you certain the bird is dead?"

Jillian looked down at the towel sadly. "It's dead."

"Let me see."

With a sigh, Jillian carefully unwrapped the crow. It lay still and far too limp in the middle of the blood-stained towel. "Judging from all the blood, I don't think there was anything I could have done, even if I'd found it when it was still alive."

"What are you doing in my room?"

At the imperious tone, Jillian jumped, and the crow rolled out of the towel and hit the floor with a muffled thud. All three women looked down at it for a moment, silent.

"I was bringing you a glass of tea." Jillian looked around, suddenly realizing she had no idea what Savannah had done with the glass of tea. *Was she carrying it when she left?* Jillian couldn't remember.

"With a crow? I prefer a lemon garnish."

"The crow was already here. I found it in the bathroom. You don't want to go in there until I clean it up."

The actress looked pointedly at Cornelia's smoldering herb stick. "And you were going to burn the corpse? What sort of odd customs do you people have?"

Cornelia gave the actress a look of disdain. "Of course not. I was using the herbs to cleanse the spiritual atmosphere in the house. I only came in here to help Jillian determine how the crow got into your room."

"And you discovered what?"

"Nothing actually," Jillian said. "I have no idea, but I'll clean it up right now. If you want to go and have some lunch, I'll have the room completely spotless by the time you're done."

The older woman's expression made it clear that she was not happy with the situation at all. "I know this is an older home, and I like that about it, but I simply cannot abide vermin."

"I'm sure we don't have a crow infestation," Jillian said. "Could this be someone's idea of a joke?"

The actress folded her arms over her chest and stared down at the dead crow. "Some of the young people in this movie crew do have an appalling lack of respect for their elders. Still, I cannot imagine who would find that amusing." Then she narrowed her eyes. "Perhaps some of those dreadful protesters have gotten in the house. That kind of person would do almost anything."

"Maybe," Jillian said. "Though the sheriff put a pretty bad scare in them when he came out yesterday. I don't think they'd come up to the house."

"I do think we have to consider the obvious answer," Cornelia said.

Stifling a groan. Jillian turned to her aunt. Whenever Cornelia thought something was obvious, the answer tended to be the same. Jillian suddenly wished she had a magical way to keep Cornelia from saying what she surely intended. "Why don't we just get the room cleaned up?"

"What is the obvious answer?" the actress asked. For just an instant, as the two older women faced one another with intent expressions, Jillian was struck by how similar they were. At nearly the same height, they were both petite, small-boned women with erect postures that belied their years. The main difference between them was Cornelia's fluff of blond curls and the actress's constant sour expression.

Her aunt's voice pulled her attention back to the unfortunate conversation. "The haint is sending us a message, of course. You movie people are using the grounds to tell a ghost story, so the Belle Haven haint is simply making her presence known. She probably doesn't like being shunted to the side by some pretend ghost. I really should have foreseen that before you let the movie crew come here, Jillian."

Jillian stared at her aunt in shock. *When did the horror movie turn into my idea?*

Nearly a month ago, Cornelia had been out at the Moss Hollow cemetery communing with the spirits or some such, and while she was there, she'd met the location scout for *Deadly Gothic*. When she had heard they were looking for a plantation for the film setting, it was Cornelia herself who had invited them to check out Belle Haven.

Gloria Baxter's gravelly voice tugged Jillian's attention away from her personal outrage. "I'll leave you both to clean my room. And air it out. I can't stand the smell of smoke. It's making my sinuses itch. I'll be down in the living room. You can bring me a glass of tea there." She turned and swept out of the room.

"I can't believe you, Aunt Cornelia. *You're* the one who brought the location scout out here to the house." Jillian bent to wrap up the dead crow in the towel again.

Cornelia sniffed. "That was a small misjudgment on my part, but I was ready to run him off when he referred to my garden as *creepy!*"

"I think he only meant the overgrown parts, not the front gardens, which are beautiful."

"He didn't specify."

"Plus, you seemed eager enough to have them here last night when you came downstairs in tap shoes to show Christopher Dark how spry you are."

"Graceful," Cornelia said. "Not spry. But the man has no taste in hiring, since it's surely one of the people he hired who put that poor crow in the bathroom. I'm surprised the person didn't put it in the director's room in protest against that ridiculous vest he wears everywhere."

"Fine. Christopher Dark has no taste. But the film crew is here now, and we need the money." Jillian stood back up. "I'll take this outside. You should get rid of that smoking thing. And please, open the windows in here. I'll come up and scrub the bathroom floor as soon as I get rid of the bird and get Gloria her tea."

She carried the blood-stained bundle outside, going out through the front of the house to avoid passing anyone who might be trying to eat. The view from the front veranda of Belle Haven gave no suggestion of the overgrown mess that made up so much of the back property, though the sight of the small knot of people carrying signs at the edge of the property didn't cheer her up much. At least she couldn't read the signs from so far away.

She pointedly turned her attention to the manicured garden that her aunt had turned into a work of art. The front gardens were perfectly tended and bursting with summer color. The director had grumbled a bit about not being able to use the front in any establishing shots, but Jillian had put a quick end to his ideas about "roughing up the place a little."

She stepped off the veranda on the right side of the house where it wrapped around for a short distance and offered an outside entry into the Belle Haven library. Dusty, dismal, and musty-smelling, the two-story library had once been an incredible room, but those days were well before Jillian's lifetime. Now the kindest thing that could be said about it was that the gas fireplace still worked, though it was rarely used. In its present state, the library was to be the location for many of the movie's interior shots.

As she walked, the trees on the side of the house offered a nice bit of shade. She had hired some local guys to cut dead limbs and give all the trees some care so they looked lush instead of neglected. Following the trees to the back of the property, the underbrush grew denser as she continued deeper into the grounds. The soil grew softer underfoot and she knew she was in the wetlands section. This was an area she planned to leave undisturbed during any future updates since she knew wetlands were important to the ecology and far too often destroyed by eager homeowners.

Deep in the shadowy brush, Jillian gently unwrapped the bird. "I'm sorry I couldn't help you," she whispered as she knelt and rolled it out onto the ground. As the dead bird flopped onto its back, Jillian finally saw the wound that had killed it. The bird had a huge gash in its chest that looked anything but natural. "How did you get that?" Since neither bird nor Cornelia's imaginary haint answered her, she finally stood and shook out the stained towel before folding it up carefully to hide the blood stains. She'd go ahead and throw it in the washer, then grab some rags from the laundry room before getting Gloria her tea and heading back upstairs to clean the bathroom.

Since the laundry room was easiest to access from the *porte cochere* off the other end of the house, Jillian waded out of the brush and into the overgrown garden area. This was another part of Belle Haven that had been magnificent in the distant past. She followed a barely discernible path back toward the house, but paused when she heard raised voices, recognizing one immediately as the gravelly tones of Gloria Baxter. Apparently the actress wasn't waiting in the living room after all. She must have gone right outside after talking to Jillian.

Jillian crept forward, curious to know with whom Gloria was fighting. Could it be the person who left the dead crow in her room? Finally she could see two people ahead near the old fountain that hadn't held water in decades.

"Don't play games with me, girl," Gloria commanded.

The young woman standing opposite Gloria crossed her arms over her chest and drew back her shoulders. Jillian could see her clearly now. It was Annika Venn, though the twisted scowl made her look far different from her usual bright, cheerful self. "Me playing games? You invented the mind game, lady, and I'm not interested in whatever you've got going."

"I know you put that bird in our bathroom."

"What bird?" Annika threw her hands in the air. "You're not making any sense. You don't make sense about half the time, and don't think we haven't all noticed how often you forget your lines. Maybe you should have that checked. Senility is a terrible thing."

"I am not senile," Gloria snapped. "I see clearly, I think clearly, and I see a terribly jealous young woman whose career will never reach the heights that mine has achieved."

"What heights? I never even heard of you until my agent got me this gig."

"I was a star when you were wetting your diapers, child."

"And I'll be a star when you're barely a bad memory of bad acting in bad movies," Annika snapped.

Jillian was shocked by the last remark. Although Gloria Baxter could test the temperament of anyone, she'd not thought Annika was the sort to go for such a scathing remark. She coughed to signal her presence then walked on out into the clearing that held the fountain.

"Did you both have enough lunch?" Jillian asked pleasantly. "I believe there are some scones left."

"No thanks. I'm about fed up," Annika said, then spun on her heel and stalked out of the garden.

The older actress watched her go through narrowed eyes. "I thought you were cleaning my room."

"I'm heading up to your room to scrub the floor now," Jillian said. "It should be good to go in about five minutes. Do you still want some tea in the living room when I'm done?"

"Of course."

It wouldn't kill you to say please. Jillian forced down her inner snarky voice and just smiled and nodded. She wondered if the crow really was someone's idea of a practical joke. She hoped not. The death of an innocent creature wasn't funny in the slightest.

Once Gloria stalked off, Jillian hurried to the laundry room to throw the towel into the washing machine. She was surprised to find Bibi at the laundry sink, washing her hands. "Do you need anything?"

Bibi's face flushed. "No, I just slapped some kind of biting fly and got it on my hands." She shuddered. "I had to get it off right away. I know it's silly, but I just hate anything dirty. And there are so very many insects here. I'm sorry if this room is off-limits."

Jillian smiled at her. "Only the private family rooms are off-limits. You're welcome to wash your hands in here any time you like." She handed Bibi a towel from the basket of clean towels on the laundry room counter.

"Thanks." Bibi quickly scrubbed at her hands and handed the towel back. "Sorry." Then she practically ran out of the room.

Jillian stared after her for a moment, wondering if the woman was always that tightly wound, or if it was working for Gloria that made her that way. As she turned back to her task and poured some stain treatment on the bloody towel, she thought again about the wound on the crow's chest. It looked more like a stab wound than something the bird might have gotten accidentally. Of course, if it did fly through a broken window, a shard of glass could have stabbed it as easily as a knife. It really was too soon to be sure someone had hurt the bird on purpose, though she couldn't imagine how a dead bird could end up on Gloria Baxter's bathroom floor without help.

After leaving the stained towel to soak, Jillian scrubbed her hands in the laundry room sink until they were bright pink, then she walked into the kitchen. When she saw the film crew still sitting at a table in the breakfast room, she realized she'd need to let those staying at Belle Haven know that she would be checking their rooms for broken windows. She saw Annika was back at the table with the others, laughing and flicking ice cubes at her co-star, Kane Porter. Without the ax or the vicious expression, Kane looked as harmless as Annika herself.

At the end of the table, the director sat silently, seemingly lost in thought as he finished up a small salad for his lunch.

"Excuse me?" Jillian said. "I'm sorry to interrupt, but it appears that a large bird has flown into one of the upstairs windows and broken it. I'm not certain which window so I'll need to go into every room." She looked directly at Annika, Kane, and the director. "I won't disturb any of your things. I simply need to check the windows."

Annika turned an interested look toward Jillian. "That's fine," Annika said. "Is that the bird Gloria was going on and on about?"

"Yes," Jillian said.

Kane's expression turned concerned. "Is the bird all right? I hate it when birds hit windows. We have a beach house back in California and birds smack into all that glass all the time. It's brutal."

"The bird didn't survive."

"What kind of bird was it?" the director asked, his expression intense but unreadable.

Jillian turned to him, surprised. "A crow. Why?"

The man shrugged, then smiled grimly. "Just wondering. You haven't seen the shooting script?"

Jillian shook her head. "I like to stay focused on food and lodging."

"Later in the movie, there's a crow. Annika's character kills it."

"But I don't really." Annika patted Kane's arm. "It's all done with computers now. The animal rights folks would have our heads if we actually hurt a bird."

"And we'd deserve it," Kane said. "I've read about all the terrible things they used to do to real animals in the movies. I wouldn't be part of anything like that."

"You're such a big softie," Annika said.

"Of course we would never injure a bird," Christopher said. He took a long sip of his iced tea, his eyes on Annika.

Kane turned toward the director with a narrowed gaze. "You realize that birds didn't voluntarily give up their feathers for that vest, nor did the cow offer up its hide."

Annika whistled, clearly surprised that Kane had brought that up.

The director pointed a coffee spoon at Kane. "I'm not discussing my vest with you."

Jillian decided that film people were just plain weird. She thanked them for their attention and turned to leave the kitchen. Bertie caught her on the way out. "Is there a dead crow in my house?"

"Not anymore," Jillian whispered back. "I took care of it. But I have to get upstairs and do some cleaning."

Bertie wrinkled her nose. "Fine. I'll clean up here and then head back to the bakery. I hope I can resist the urge to run over some protesters on my way out. Can you handle the afternoon snacks? I'll be back for supper."

"You don't need to clean up. I can handle it all. If I need help, I can always ask Aunt Cornelia."

Bertie rolled her eyes. "Sure you can. My sister has gotten even more woo-woo since this movie stuff started. If she thinks that's going to sway the director into giving her a role, she needs to think again."

"Maybe we should think of a way to get Cornelia out of the house for a while and give her something else to think about besides the movie," Jillian said.

"Good idea," Bertie agreed, surprising Jillian. Her grandmother so rarely agreed with her about anything. "I'll call right now and see if Jasmine over at the Clip & Curl can get us in this afternoon. Cornelia and I can have our hair done. Maybe our nails too."

The surprise at that nearly bowled Jillian over. Her grandmother tended to treat the hairdresser as a necessary evil, going only when her hair threatened to flop into her eyes. And she was pretty sure Bertie had never had her nails professionally done in her life.

Bertie scowled at her. "Don't look at me that way. I can care about my looks like anyone else."

A slow smile spread across Jillian's face. "And the timing wouldn't have anything to do with the interest of a certain cowboy?"

"Don't talk foolishness," Bertie said and flapped a dish towel at Jillian. "You said you had something to clean upstairs. You best get on it."

Jillian was still chuckling as she grabbed a glass of iced tea, intending to give it to Gloria before heading upstairs. She walked into the living room and found a young man reading in one of the comfortable chairs, but no sign of the actress. She vaguely recognized him as one of the crew members who seemed to be forever moving cables around. When she asked the young man if he'd seen Gloria, he shook his head briefly and returned to his book. With an annoyed huff, Jillian left the glass on the coffee table, resting on a coaster. "If Gloria comes in, please tell her that's her tea." The young man bobbed his head without looking up.

After that, Jillian headed upstairs to her grisly cleanup chore. She certainly hoped that leaving a dead bird wasn't someone's idea of a joke, but she didn't see any other way it could have ended up in that bathroom. She stopped at the hall closet on the second floor and grabbed some spray cleaner.

When she opened the door to Gloria Baxter's room, she half-expected to see Cornelia, still wafting smoke, but her aunt had opened the bedroom windows and left. Only the vaguest hint of earthy sage smoke remained, and it had faded until it was actually pleasant, though Jillian didn't want any lingering traces around to give Gloria something to complain about. She walked to the closet and grabbed the small fan she'd put in each of the rooms in case the actors weren't cool enough. She plugged it in and set the fan on a table so it could pull air from the room and out the window.

Having done all she could to put off dealing with the bloody mess, Jillian headed into the bathroom. As soon as she opened the door, she caught sight of movement and jumped before realizing she was just seeing her own reflection in the bathroom mirror. "I'm a big chicken," she muttered, then turned her attention to the blood on the floor.

Jillian froze.

The puddle of blood was smeared, but not just by the dying crow's thrashing. Someone had been in the bathroom after Jillian had removed the bird and had written in the blood in block printing. The four letters spelled out "Hexe."

Jillian stared at the disturbing message. Could the person who wrote it have been interrupted in the middle of the writing? As far as she knew, "Hexe" wasn't a word, though it sounded ominous. *I wonder if it's supposed to be "Hex,"* she thought. *Maybe someone thinks they are casting some kind of evil spell.*

She pulled her cell phone out of her pocket and took a photo of the bloody printing, making a mental note to look up the definition of "Hexe" on the Internet later. Then she knelt and washed the word and the stain from the floor. The grout between the tiles needed a lot of scrubbing, but eventually Jillian had all but the faintest discoloration gone.

As she stood back up, her knees creaking, there was a knock and the opposite door to the bathroom opened and Annika peeked in. "Hi. I heard someone in here and thought it might be Gloria. I wanted to see if I could smooth things over with her. She's such a prickly old bird."

Her choice of wording made Jillian wince. "I'm sure she's challenging to work with sometimes."

Annika laughed. "We all are sometimes."

"Since you're here, do you mind if I check your windows really quick?" Jillian asked. "I'm certain we have a broken window up here somewhere. I don't know any other way a bird could have ended up in this bathroom."

"Sure, come on in." Annika stepped out of the doorway. "I certainly don't need a broken window letting in birds, bugs, and who knows what else."

Jillian paused, suddenly remembering she still wasn't sure

what had happened to the glass of iced tea Savannah had carried up earlier. She glanced around the room, but there was no sign of a glass. She did spot a faint ring of water on the vanity and quickly wiped it away.

"You coming?" Annika asked.

"Sorry. Coming."

Because they were hosting so many people, Jillian had turned her aunt's small crafting room into another bedroom temporarily after bringing down a lovely old brass bed from third-floor storage. That's the room Annika was using. It was quite a bit smaller than Gloria's bedroom, but since Gloria's room had to fit the rollaway bed for Bibi, the larger room seemed necessary. The older actress had made note of the difference in size and reacted to it as if the room assignment were a reflection of her importance in the movie, lording it proudly over Annika.

Jillian was just grateful none of the other actors had demanded larger rooms to compete. The bathroom and two bedrooms looked out over the back porch, as did Cornelia's room on the same side of the house. The rooms that the director and Kane Porter were using were on the other side of the house and looked out over the well-tended front yard. The room Jillian was using was tucked on the end of the house, over the porte cochere.

Jillian stepped into the room and saw Annika's personal housekeeping style was the exact opposite of Gloria's. The room looked as if it had been the target of a thorough search. Every drawer of the highboy was open at least a crack, and clothes of one sort or another covered most of the surfaces. Though the deal with the filmmakers didn't include maid service, Jillian felt an overwhelming urge to tidy up.

"I know," Annika said with a giggle at Jillian's expression. "I'm a mess."

Jillian crossed the room, being careful not to step on any clothes. "I've seen worse." She couldn't think of when, but she was sure she must have. At least there was no blood in Annika's room. She pulled back the curtains, but the window was closed and unbroken.

Jillian checked the next window and saw it was unbroken as well. "Annika, does the word 'h-e-x-e' mean anything to you?"

"Of course."

Jillian turned sharply to look at the younger woman in surprise, and Annika smiled. "I may pretend not to know anything about Gloria, but I actually know the titles of all her movies. Don't tell her, but I lied. She was actually one of my idols until I met the hateful old witch."

"*Hexe* was a movie?" Jillian said.

Annika nodded. "'Hexe' means witch in German, though the movie was set in Pennsylvania, not Germany. Anyway, Gloria played the innocent girl accused of being a witch after she goes in search of her roots or some such. The villagers all treat her horribly and that unleashes her power. Mayhem ensues. It wasn't a great movie, but Gloria was amazing in it. It basically launched her career."

"That's interesting. Do you think anyone else in the crew knows about *Hexe*?"

Annika laughed as she followed Jillian to the last window. "Only everyone. Like I said, it launched Gloria's career, which was kind of amazing because she was never supposed to have the role in the first place."

Jillian pulled open the curtain, and the trapped heat behind the curtain made her flinch, but the glass was intact. The window was open a crack at the top. The old windows tended to do that if they weren't locked; the top sash would slip down. She pushed it back up and locked the window. "What happened that gave Gloria the part?"

"The star died. Technically, Gloria killed her, though it was a freak accident on the set. Gloria was part of a large group of extras that was supposed to attack the star with prop knives and clubs in a hazy dream sequence. One of the prop knives got mixed up with a real knife, and the dream sequence turned way real."

"That's horrible. How could something like that happen?"

"In films with really low budgets, so many people have to cover more than one job. That leaves room for accidents. Anyway, the director picked Gloria out of the group of extras and gave her the main character role so he could finish the movie. And thus movie history was made." Annika bounced on her toes. "Looks like I don't have any broken windows. You going to check the rest of the rooms? Can I come with?"

"I thought Christopher intended to do more outdoor filming after lunch."

"That was the original plan, but he gave in to Gloria *again*. Honestly, the old crone should only take indoor roles. At any rate, they're setting up in the library for a scene with Gloria and Kane. I'm not in it. The way Gloria has been screwing up her lines and blaming it on other people, they won't get through this scene filming until suppertime, so I'm free. Can I come help you check windows?"

"If you like. I can't promise it will be exciting."

"Of course it will," Annika said. "I love having a peek inside all these rooms. This old place is amazing. I've been a good guest and minded my own business, but that doesn't mean I'm not curious. Do you have any secret passages or hidden rooms?"

"Not as far as I know," Jillian said.

"Too bad. Hey, maybe we'll discover one."

"While we're checking windows?" Jillian was beginning to think the young actress was as fanciful as Aunt Cornelia.

"You never know." Annika followed Jillian from room to room, keeping up a cheerful chatter, which distracted Jillian from what she really wanted to do: ponder the strange message written in blood. Clearly the message was for Gloria, not Annika, and it probably would have freaked out the older actress if she'd seen it. But did it have a darker purpose other than to upset her?

She tapped on the door to Cornelia's room, but her aunt didn't answer. Maybe Bertie really *had* taken her out for an afternoon at Jasmine's Clip & Curl. She opened the door, and Annika cried out behind her. "There you are, you little sweetie."

The actress slipped around Jillian and hurried over to Cornelia's bed to coo and fuss over Possum. Technically, Possum was Bertie's cat, but he had claimed Cornelia on the day she moved in and the two were nearly inseparable. Bertie insisted Possum's devotion was entirely because of the bacon her sister gave the chubby cat every chance she got. Cornelia had a stranger theory, namely that Possum was the present repository for her late husband's spirit.

Jillian's theory was that Aunt Cornelia was a darling, slightly flaky woman who missed her late husband horribly. She watched as Annika scooped the cat off the bed and cradled him like a baby. Then the young actress looked around the room. "Your aunt certainly likes flowers."

"That she does." Aunt Cornelia was an amazing gardener, and a huge floral arrangement graced the center of her dresser, but floral patterns also covered the bedspread, the curtains, and the upholstery on her vanity chair. Jillian found it a little overwhelming, but if her aunt was happy, she was happy. She crossed to the window and pulled back the curtain. The window was intact, as were the remaining window in the room and the window in Cornelia's bathroom, where more floral patterns graced the shower curtain, bath mat, towels, and accessories.

When they walked back out to the hall, Jillian pointed at Possum. "You'd best leave him in Cornelia's room. If they're filming in the library, Possum will want to be part of it. He loves that room. I suspect it has mice."

"If you have mousetraps in there, don't tell Kane. He's against killing *anything.*" Annika reluctantly put Possum down, and Jillian thought the cat looked slightly relieved. Cornelia doted on him, but she wasn't prone to baby talk the way Annika was.

Annika closed the door to Cornelia's room. "I know the library is two stories. Is that the access from up here?" She pointed toward the mahogany door that matched the double doors on the first floor level of the library.

Jillian nodded. "That door opens onto the second-floor library balcony. It runs above three sides of the library. If you go in there, be careful of the railing. I think it should be fine, but we haven't started remodeling that yet, so I wouldn't lean heavily on it."

"I'll be careful," Annika sang out as she hurried toward the door.

"Are you sure you should go there now?" Jillian asked. "I'm certain the director will be upset if the filming is disturbed."

"We won't disturb them. None of the cameras will be pointing up, and we'll be quiet as the mice that live there."

Jillian trailed along behind her. The silence in the library was absolute. They peered over the balcony rail and saw the huge library was empty of people, though there were still plenty of lights and other equipment in the room. For the filming, the director had decided to use most of the shabby overstuffed leather furniture, though he'd ordered it moved around. Since the faded old rugs then showed the marks of the missing furniture, they'd been rolled up and piled in a corner.

When Jillian had first showed him the big room, Christopher clucked over the two stories of stuffed bookshelves. Too many of the titles were new and cheap, so they didn't match the ancient look he wanted from the room. He'd sent his property master to remove any book that might conflict with the look he wanted. Jillian saw the boxes of books tucked under the rolled-up rugs.

Someone had turned on the green-shaded desk lamp atop a cherry wood desk and the three Tiffany lamps on various small tables, giving the room a shadowy, old-fashioned glow, but the huge film lights were all off.

"I guess they finished early." *Which probably explains why Gloria didn't wait in the living room for her tea.*

"They can't have finished early," Annika said. "Not with the way Gloria has been forgetting her lines. It takes forever to film her scenes. They shouldn't be done." She pointed toward the corner where a metal spiral staircase led down to the lower floor. "Is that staircase safe?"

Jillian winced. "I don't know. I wouldn't use it."

Annika rolled her eyes at Jillian's caution. "I'm going to go down and look around the library." She spun on her heel and headed out of the library and down the main staircase. Jillian followed, intending to check the library windows for breaks, but she was more than a little curious about the change in filming too.

"If Christopher wanted to do the outside filming after all, he should have told me," Annika said when they reached the first floor and found the library doors wide open but no one inside. "I'm not going out and hunting for them."

Jillian looked over the heavy drapes covering the two tall library windows. The drapes were designed to keep out the sunlight, which faded furniture and books alike, though Jillian preferred the light even if it was hard on the furniture. When they finally restored this room, she planned to have plenty of light streaming in the windows.

She pulled back the drape on the first window and found the window unbroken, then walked by the door leading onto the veranda to get to the other window. If the bird had broken one of the library windows, it would have had access to the second floor that way, though someone would have had to leave the library door open. She could picture that easily enough with all the comings and goings of the crew. Of course, that would mean a badly injured bird flew up that far, and it seemed unlikely. *If a bird did break through a window, would it even be able to get around the heavy drapes?*

Jillian lifted the heavy drape away from the second window, raising embarrassing puffs of dust in the process, but not finding any damage. Annika stood in the middle of the room with her arms crossed and an annoyed expression on her face.

When Jillian finished checking for broken windows, she saw that the young actress had added tapping her foot to her impatient stance. "Maybe your friends are still in the breakfast room," Jillian suggested.

"Co-workers. Not friends." Annika pulled out her cell phone to check the time. "I can't see Christopher letting all this time go to waste, but no one tried to call me back to the set. I'll go outside to check, but that's it. I'm not wandering around hunting them down." Together they turned to head through the house.

When they reached the breakfast room, it was empty. Everyone had finished with lunch, and the buffet table definitely needed her attention. Apparently Bertie had taken her at her word and left. Jillian decided to clean up first and finish checking windows later. As she began picking up stray plates of half-eaten food, Annika headed outside without remark.

Jillian carried the plates into the kitchen and set them beside the sink where the mugs she'd gathered earlier still waited to be loaded into the dishwasher. She washed her hands so she could change out the table from lunch buffet to snacks. The craft services contract they'd signed agreed to provide some kind of food during all hours when the crew was filming, but full-meal catering only had to be provided within normal meal hours. That requirement had kept her out of the bakery for a couple of days, and she was surprised to find that she actually missed it. *That was something I wouldn't have believed a year ago!*

Cleaning up the lunch buffet and refreshing the table with snacks and drinks took all of Jillian's attention for a while, though the image of the word written in blood on the bathroom tiles came back to her several times. She hoped that whoever thought up something so gruesome was done with pranks.

She'd just finished filling up the tall iced-coffee dispenser when Leo Shone came in, mopping his brow with a handkerchief. "I thought Texas was hot," he said to Jillian, "but y'all have cornered the market on natural sauna."

"Georgia in the summer is a challenge," Jillian answered. "Be sure to stay hydrated. That's really the key to surviving it."

"I'll keep that in mind." He opened the cooler on the table and fished out an icy bottle of water, rubbing it across his forehead.

"Are they still filming in the garden?" Jillian asked.

Leo shook his head. "They aren't filming at all. Everyone's looking for Gloria. The old girl has wandered off somewhere, and Christopher is furious. She best be careful. She's costing the film an arm and a leg with all her diva antics. Chris won't put up with that forever."

"I wonder where she is," Jillian said. "She wasn't upstairs, and I didn't see her when I came down either." Of course, she hadn't searched all the downstairs rooms, but she couldn't imagine the actress hiding in the office or Bertie's suite of rooms. Then she remembered the promised iced tea. "Oh, maybe Gloria is in the living room. She said something earlier about going there."

Leo shrugged as he unscrewed the cap on the water bottle and chugged down about half the contents before answering.

"Fine, I'll check in a minute. Though if she's been sitting around soaking up the air-conditioning while we've been looking for her, Christopher is going to blow a blood vessel."

"You wait here. I'll check." As she came around the counter, Jillian caught sight of movement through one of the French doors that led to the back porch. One of the crew members burst in. "Christopher says to call 911. It's Ms. Baxter. I think she's dead!"

4

"**D**ead!" Jillian rushed to the phone in the kitchen. "Are you sure? What happened?"

"I don't know," the young crewman said. His hair stuck to his head in sweaty hanks, and his skin grayed with anxiety. "I didn't see her. But Christopher looked really upset, and he said she was bleeding."

So maybe not dead. "You should get some water." Jillian pointed toward the craft services tables while the phone connected her. Then she turned her full attention to the emergency operator. She couldn't answer many of the woman's questions, basically just saying an older woman was in need of emergency medical attention and giving the address for Belle Haven. "I don't know anything else. I haven't seen her, but you should hurry. Tell them the woman is around the back of the house. They should be able to pull around through the porte cochere."

"Got it. Someone is on the way," the operator assured her.

As soon as she hung up, Jillian turned back to the breakfast room. She saw that Leo had gone on outside, while the young crewman sat at one of the tables in the breakfast room, sipping from a bottle of water with shaking hands. "Where is everyone?"

The crewman pointed vaguely toward the backyard with the water bottle. "Gloria was in some little shed thing back there."

Belle Haven had a number of outbuildings, though most were completely unused and probably more than a little unsafe. With the money they'd make from *Deadly Gothic*, she'd hoped to clean up the back garden all the way to the old tobacco barn and renovate the large building for events. So far, that was only a dream. Jillian hadn't even had the nerve to check out the barn to see if it was in good enough condition to be renovated. At any rate, she was sure no one would describe the big barn as a little shed, so it must be one of the smaller buildings.

As she stepped outside, the heat and humidity slapped her in the face again like a wet towel. She wondered if Gloria had simply had too much heat. Heatstroke wasn't exactly rare in Georgia in the middle of summer, especially if the older woman hadn't been hydrating properly.

She crossed the well-tended part of the back lawn, noting a few places where the heavy camera equipment and the passage of many feet were beginning to wear on the grass. At least it had been a wet summer so far, which means the grass rebounded well from the abuse. *What am I doing thinking about grass when someone is injured or worse?* Jillian gave herself a mental shake.

Beyond the lawn, paving stones formed a small patio at the edge of the back flower gardens. Cornelia and her garden club had slowly been reclaiming the formal gardens at the back of the house, but a good half of the space was still overgrown and every bit as creepy as the location scout had declared it. Hurrying down the garden path, Jillian found the change from tended to wild garden striking.

She circled the large fountain topped by the statue of a young woman, her serene face marred by splotches of lichen. Jillian hoped to have the fountain restored. She sighed as she pushed deeper down the overgrown path. There were so many things on her list of hopeful changes. The thick undergrowth hid thorny roses and other hazards, as well as being home to swarms of buzzing, biting gnats. Jillian flapped a hand to drive the tiny creatures away from her face.

Up ahead she heard voices. She practically had to bushwhack for the last bit, shoving aside branches and stomping brush to burst through to the clearing where one of the shabbier outbuildings stood. The clearing was full of people, pressed almost shoulder to shoulder as they crowded the front of the small shed.

"I've called for an ambulance," Jillian said. "But I didn't know how to describe Miss Baxter's injury."

"I'm not injured!" The actress's voice was slightly shaky, and Jillian still could not see her through the crowd, but she felt a rush of relief at the sound of her voice.

"We'll need to make room for the emergency crew," Jillian suggested. "I can watch for them and direct them back this way when they arrive, but I need to know what to tell them."

The crowd reluctantly shifted to make way for Jillian to step through. She saw Gloria Baxter seated on the ground with her assistant crouched next to her, dabbing at Gloria's forehead with a handkerchief. The handkerchief and much of the actress's face were covered in blood, reminding Jillian of the puddle she'd just cleaned up in Gloria's bathroom. "What happened?" she cried.

"I got a little turned around," Gloria snapped. "The brush back here is very confusing. I saw the shed and hoped I would find something to help me get back to the house, but I tripped and hit my head. It's nothing. It's ridiculous to call an ambulance."

"It isn't nothing," Bibi Bleu insisted. "You've been hurt, and it could've been a lot worse."

"I'm afraid I have to insist you be seen by a doctor," Christopher Dark said, his expression well matching his name as he scowled down at the actress with his arms crossed, a gesture which sent one of the feathers from his vest floating to the ground. "The insurance company would have a fit if you weren't."

"Fine," the actress snapped. "But it's all quite ridiculous."

"I'm sorry you got lost," Jillian said. "Why didn't you call anyone?"

"I'm not a foghorn, and I don't carry around a phone. I think they're rather vulgar," the actress said, turning her angry eyes toward Jillian. "I do wish you would all let me walk back to the house at least. The insects back here are terrible. I could end up with malaria while you're making me sit in the dirt."

"Do you think you can stand?" Bibi asked.

"If someone would give me a hand."

Two of the younger crew members rushed to haul the old woman to her feet where she teetered a bit. "Are you dizzy?" Jillian asked. "You could have a concussion."

"I don't have a concussion," the actress snapped. "I just haven't eaten. And sitting out here in the heat isn't helping. I want to be inside where it's cooler."

"That might be wise," Jillian said. "Heatstroke wouldn't make her feel any better."

"If she's feeling woozy, I could carry her." Everyone turned to look at Kane Porter, who shrugged his well-muscled shoulders. "She isn't very big. I used to work with my uncle building houses. I've picked up stuff way heavier than her."

Gloria glared in the young actor's direction. "That person isn't to touch me. None of them are. It's in my contract." Jillian saw the expression on the young actor's face, a mixture of surprise and hurt.

"Stop arguing." Christopher Dark pointed at a broad-shouldered young man that Jillian had seen carrying heavy equipment. She didn't know his name. "Carry her back to the house."

The crewman took a step toward Gloria, but she held up a bloodstained hand. "I told you already that no one is to carry me. I can walk."

And so the whole group headed slowly back toward the mansion. With the excitement passing, some of the crew trotted on ahead, clearly having had enough of the gnats in the thickets. Jillian was reluctant to leave the actress, who leaned heavily on her assistant's arm as she negotiated the overgrown paths, but she knew someone needed to meet the ambulance.

She was still trying to decide when Bibi turned toward her, fury written all over her round face. "The paths need to be marked somehow."

Jillian looked at her in surprise. "Wouldn't that be a problem for the filming? It's supposed to look wild and overgrown."

"Sure." The assistant's voice was thick with sarcasm. "Looks are so much more important than Miss Baxter's health."

"Stop that foolish chattering, Bibi," Gloria said. "You know how your voice grates on my nerves when I have a headache."

"Of course, Miss Baxter," Bibi said softly, but she still sent Jillian another angry glare.

Jillian had had enough ill-tempered glares. "I'll run ahead so I can direct the ambulance. There's water on ice in the breakfast room, which should help Miss Baxter cool down."

"I'll handle it," Bibi said, offering another nasty look.

Fine. Jillian left them behind as she stomped out of the garden as quickly as possible. She'd just made it to the back lawn when she heard the sound of sirens. Her mood improved as she thought of handing off the mess to someone else.

She walked through the house to meet the ambulance on the drive. To her surprise, the ambulance seemed to be just the beginning of the parade. The short emergency tech truck from the Moss Hollow Volunteer Fire Department pulled in right behind the ambulance, followed by a Nathan County sheriff's car and Aunt Cornelia's meticulously restored powder-blue Mustang fastback. Her aunt and grandmother jumped out of the car the moment it stopped. "What's going on?" Bertie demanded.

Jillian was distracted for a moment by Bertie's head of soft blonde curls. Her grandmother had never looked so much like her sister before, and it took Jillian by surprise. "Your hair is really nice."

Bertie flapped a hand, which drew Jillian's attention to the neat manicure. "Never mind about my hair. Why do we have an ambulance here?"

"Did you fall down the stairs again?" Cornelia asked, peering at Jillian in concern.

Jillian huffed. "Once. I fell down the stairs once. It's not my hobby."

"Who fell down the stairs?" An emergency tech hurried toward them with heavy cases in each hand.

"Was the person pushed?" This last came from Deputy Goodman Jones. The deputy had a low opinion of Jillian. He seemed to think catastrophe followed her around just because she'd gotten caught up in a few situations since moving back to Moss Hollow.

"No one fell down the stairs," Jillian said. "And no one was pushed. One of our guests fell in the garden and hit her head. Follow me." She led the parade of emergency workers, relatives, and the deputy down the drive, through the porte cochere and into the house, leaving the two ambulance drivers to unload the stretcher and follow after them.

As Jillian led her group into the breakfast room, Gloria hobbled in, still leaning heavily on Bibi. The older woman's silver hair was matted to her head with blood and her skin was pale as milk. The emergency worker practically ran to her side. "You shouldn't be on your feet," he scolded as he helped the actress to the closest chair.

"Rubbish," Gloria said, though her voice was slightly wheezy from the long walk. While the actress was poked, prodded, and asked to count raised fingers, she kept up a steady flow of complaints. Finally she pointed a crooked finger at Gooder. "You find out who put that bird in my room, you hear?"

Gooder gave Jillian a slight smile. "Bird?"

"I found a dead crow in Ms. Baxter's bathroom," she said. "It was a big crow. I think it might have flown into a window and broken the glass, though I haven't been able to find the broken window yet."

"Did you check them all?"

Jillian shook her head. "Belle Haven has a lot of windows."

"Where's the bird?"

"I disposed of it in the woods."

"Then it sounds like the case is closed," Gooder said. "Sheriff Henderson will be glad to hear that." He looked back toward the actress who had turned her attention and anger to the blood pressure cuff, which she apparently thought was too tight.

Jillian considered telling Gooder about the message written in blood on the bathroom floor, but she knew that he'd find a way to suggest it was either her doing or something she was imagining. The deputy thought she poked her nose into places it didn't belong and tended to give anything she said as little credence as possible. Finally, Jillian decided to hold off unless more pranks followed that one.

Her attention was jerked back to Gloria when the actress practically shouted, "I do not have a concussion!"

"Actually, I believe you do," the medical tech said, his voice patient. "So we're going to take you to the hospital where you can be checked out by a doctor."

"No!" Gloria insisted.

"Oh, let them take you," Christopher Dark said. "Insurance will demand it anyway before you can do any more filming. You go, and I'll send someone to bring you back as soon as they say you can."

Since she didn't have much choice, Gloria finally let them move her to the stretcher with as much grumbling as possible. When she was strapped in and ready to go, they wheeled her across into the kitchen. Gloria darted a hand out and grabbed the arm of the ambulance attendant. "Stop."

The stretcher stopped rolling and Gloria demanded that Jillian come over to speak to her. Surprised, Jillian walked over.

Gloria glared at the ambulance attendants. "Give me a little privacy, please."

"Step away," Bibi announced, rushing over to shoo the emergency crew.

"You too," Gloria said to her assistant. "This is just between her and me."

Bibi looked at her boss in surprise, then at Jillian. She clearly wasn't happy with the idea that her boss might shut her out of something, but she finally stepped away from the stretcher, though she watched them both intently.

Gloria waved Jillian over and kept waving until Jillian leaned over. "I didn't fall," the actress whispered so softly Jillian barely heard her.

Jillian was so surprised she half-raised to look into Gloria's face. "What?"

Gloria caught Jillian's blouse and pulled her back down. "Someone is trying to kill me."

Gloria let go of Jillian's clothes and sank back onto the stretcher, her eyes full of fear. Jillian didn't know what to say. She stood, slightly numb, as Bibi Bleu swept back in, practically clinging to the stretcher as it was rolled through the house.

"What did she say?" Annika asked, making Jillian jump.

"Annika! You startled me." Jillian looked at the young actress before smiling weakly. "It was private."

Annika crossed her arms over her chest and frowned. "The old bat told you to lock the door from her room to the bathroom, didn't she? She's afraid I'll poke around in her stuff." She leaned forward and whispered, "Which I totally would. But still, that's just insulting."

Jillian almost smiled at the young woman's admission, but the chill of Gloria Baxter's words hung over her. Was someone really trying to kill her or was the older woman imagining things? She had gotten lost in the backyard. Plus, there were the complaints about her forgetting lines. She could possibly be confused.

"This is definitely not a crime scene," Gooder announced to the milling group. "And as much as I like movies, I need to get back to real work." He nodded at Jillian and headed toward the side door that led out onto the porte cochere.

She watched his back for a moment, then hurried after him, catching him just outside. "Gooder?"

He sighed and turned. "Would it kill you to call me Deputy Jones?"

"Of course not. Deputy Jones, Ms. Baxter thinks someone is trying to kill her."

He raised his eyebrows. "She said she fell."

"She whispered to me that she didn't. Plus, there's the bloody crow."

"I thought you said the bird flew into a window. That's hardly a police matter."

Jillian told him about the message on the bathroom floor, but the skeptical look never left his face. He crossed his arms over his chest. "This movie they're making, it's a horror movie, right?"

"Yes, so?"

"So that all sounds like a publicity stunt to me. The scary dead bird, the message in blood, the gasped cry for help."

"She sounded genuinely scared to me."

Gooder rolled his eyes. "I would hope so. She's a professional actress. And she's old. It's got to be hard for an older lady to get roles these days."

Jillian put her hands on her hips. "I expect she's about Bertie's age. Imagine what my grandmother would do to you if she knew you called her old."

Gooder raised both hands. "Don't go siccing Bertie Harper on me. I'm just calling it like I see it."

"The gash in Ms. Baxter's head was real," Jillian said. "With real blood coming out."

"So she tripped and decided to take advantage of it by weaving it into her scary bird thing." Gooder wiped his face with his hand. "By the way, we could have had this conversation inside with the air-conditioning and a glass of iced tea."

"I wasn't sure if we should have it at all," Jillian admitted. "I assumed you wouldn't take anything I said seriously."

"I always take you seriously," Gooder said. "Sometimes it's with serious irritation, but it's always serious. And if you come up with anything that doesn't sound like a publicity stunt for a horror movie, you let me know. And if you find out who left a bird in your bathroom, you let me know that too. We have animal cruelty laws here."

Jillian knew better than to argue the point with the deputy. One thing she and Gooder had in common was a stubborn streak a mile wide. "Fine. Thanks for coming out."

"Just doing my job, ma'am. Now if you'll excuse me."

Before he could get to his car, Jillian caught sight of a small group of women, clutching signs and peering around the corner of the house while one shot photos. "Hey," she yelled. "Y'all aren't supposed to be on the property."

A tall woman, with a lined face and her hair dyed a burgundy color, stood at the front of the group. While the other members all held signs, she clutched a large camera with a fancy lens. She jutted out her chin defiantly. "We saw the ambulance and assumed your gruesome movie had produced some horrific accident, which should be a surprise to no one. That's what horror movies do. They result in damaged lives."

"That's ridiculous." Jillian turned to Gooder who stood, gazing wistfully at his car. "Deputy Jones, the sheriff told these people to stay off our property. Shouldn't you do something about them?"

"We have a right to protest," the tall woman insisted loudly. "It's in the Constitution."

"You do," Gooder agreed, "but not on private land. I'm sure the sheriff explained the rules to you. Also, these people have a right to privacy. I should seize the memory card from that camera."

"Celebrities have given up the right to privacy," the tall woman said. "I can name the court cases." She turned toward her followers, as if for support, then back toward Gooder. "How much are these horrible people paying the sheriff's department to shield them from public censure?"

Gooder narrowed his eyes. "That's not the sort of accusation you want to be making around here, ma'am. Now you can move on off the property, or I can arrest the whole lot of you for trespassing."

"Wouldn't the press love that?" the woman asked, smiling. "Harassment of private citizens exercising their constitutional rights."

At that moment, the door behind Jillian flew open and Bertie stormed out, stomping over to the much taller protester and glaring up at her. "There is no constitutional right to tromp all over my land and make a general nuisance of yourselves. Now git, before we turn the dogs loose on you."

The woman turned to Gooder. "Did you hear this woman threaten me?"

"That's it!" the deputy shouted. "I'm getting my extra cuffs from the car." He turned to Bertie. "Can I commandeer the bakery van? I don't think I can get all of them into my car."

Bertie folded her arms over her chest, a satisfied expression on her face. To Jillian's surprise, the tall leader of the protesters did the same. She smiled at Gooder's expression. "Go ahead."

"Collette." A slender woman about Jillian's age stepped closer to the leader, fiddling with the handle of her sign nervously. "I don't want to be arrested. I don't believe my husband would like that."

"Mine neither," chirped one of the other women. "He barely let me come with you in the first place."

"Let's just go back to the edge of the property," a third urged. "Oh yes, let's."

The group backed away from their leader, then turned and hurried off. Collette seemed so shocked by the desertion that she didn't speak for a moment. Then she spun to face the deputy. "Well, I'm not intimidated by any of you."

"Not a problem," he said cheerfully as he pulled out a pair of handcuffs and held them up before smiling in Bertie's direction. "I won't need the van after all."

The abandoned leader seemed to think about it for a moment, then turned without speaking and stomped after her followers.

"Y'all do add such unique moments to my workday," Gooder said as he put away the cuffs.

"Don't be so sassy," Bertie said. "You get on about your work."

"Yes ma'am." The deputy headed for his car, looking much cheerier, but he turned back before he reached the door. "Have y'all gotten dogs, Miss Bertie?"

"Of course not. But I might've sicced Possum on them."

Gooder chuckled and opened the car door, wincing as trapped heat rolled out at him.

Jillian followed her grandmother back inside where she saw nearly the whole crew lounging at tables. "You should get some snacks out. I'll finish the cleanup."

Catching the note of reproof in her grandmother's tone, Jillian protested. "It's been a little busy around here."

"I'm sure," Bertie said. "But I still need to get to the bakery, so let's get this cleaned up."

Bertie headed straight into the kitchen and began unloading the dishwasher load that Jillian had run earlier. Leo Shone saw her and strolled over. "Let me help with those." He picked up a dish towel.

Still mildly annoyed by Bertie's tone, Jillian said, "You can go on to the bakery. I'll finish up here."

"Fine." Bertie plunked a clean mug down on the counter, provoking a disappointed look from Leo. "What did you want to talk to Gooder Jones about anyway?"

"I wanted to tell him the crow didn't look like an accident to me."

Leo set the towel back on the counter. "What's all this fuss about a dead crow? Where I come from, they're nothing but nuisances."

"The fuss is that someone intentionally put the bird in Gloria's bathroom. Crows don't use doorknobs. Plus, I haven't been able to find any broken glass. The deputy thinks it might have been a publicity stunt."

Leo chuckled. "If it was, it wouldn't have been hidden in Gloria's room. It would have been hanging from the pillars on the end of the driveway. That's the whole thing about publicity stunts. They aren't exactly subtle. If Christopher planned something like that, he would have dropped the crow on the protesters."

"Unless it wasn't Christopher's stunt," Jillian said. "Gooder thought it might be something Gloria cooked up to promote herself."

Leo wrinkled his nose. "I can't see Gloria handling a dead bird. Though I probably can imagine her ordering poor Bibi to do it."

"Either way, I don't need that kind of publicity around my home. It just encourages those protest hooligans," Bertie grumbled. "And I wouldn't put it past that Collette woman to have snuck into the house earlier to leave the dead bird, just to stir things up." She threw her hands into the air. "I've had about enough Hollywood for the day. Lenora is bringing over fried chicken for this bunch for dinner, and I whipped up a potato salad in the fridge. There's fruit in there, left over from breakfast, so you can put together a fruit salad too. I'm going in to the bakery for real this time. I don't want our customers to forget what I look like."

Jillian felt a surge of gratitude. Lenora Ryan had worked for Bertie so long that she felt like family, and she went above and beyond the call of duty any time they had a need. Plus, she made the best fried chicken that Jillian had ever tasted.

"Be careful on the way out," Jillian said. "Apparently those protesters threw pecans at Savannah's car earlier today."

"They didn't dare throw anything when Cornelia and I left earlier," Bertie said. "And I suspect Gooder took the wind out of their sails."

Jillian smiled at her. "Just don't run over any of them. And don't yell at Maggie when you get to the bakery."

"Now why would I yell at Maggie?" Bertie demanded.

"Because you're in a bad mood," Jillian said. "You know you do that. And we don't need to break in new counter help."

"I don't know what you're talking about. I'll see you at supper."

"You know I'd like to see that bakery," Leo said. "Since Christopher called off filming for the rest of the day, I'm free."

Bertie untied the apron from around her waist, and hung it on the peg. "Don't you need to practice your lines, or some such?"

He grinned at her. "That's the beauty of playing the strong, silent type. I don't have a lot of lines. I mostly just loom and look crazy in a handful of scenes."

Bertie frowned at him. "I reckon you can come, but the bakery isn't exactly a tourist attraction. There's not much to see."

"I love looking at baked goods," he said.

She rolled her eyes at that and turned to Jillian. "You okay here?"

"I'll be fine, as long as I don't have to fry the chicken. It's not one of my gifts."

"No problem. I just need to get there soon enough to let Lenora off early so she can fix it. I'll see you after I close up." She turned without saying anything else and headed toward the side door with Leo on her heels. Jillian grinned after them.

Almost as soon as Bertie left, Cornelia swept into the room from outside. The humidity had wilted her freshly fluffed blonde hair and her floral dress looked more limp than floaty. "I have been walking in the back gardens. The energy there is definitely unsettled."

"I'm surprised there's any energy left in this heat," Jillian said as she turned to the dishwasher and finished unloading the mugs her grandmother had abandoned.

Her aunt gave her a sharp glance as she stepped up next to Jillian and pulled out a baking sheet to use as a tray for the mugs. "You know spiritual energy doesn't work that way."

Jillian began piling the mugs on the tray. "I don't know much of anything about spiritual energy, and I'm just fine with that." Then she had a thought and froze with a mug in her hand. "Do you think Bertie is interested in Leo?"

Cornelia took the mug from her and put it on the tray. "I don't know. I think she enjoys the attention more than she'd like to admit, but I doubt she'd seriously consider a relationship with an actor."

Jillian nodded and returned to unloading the dishwasher. She wondered how she'd feel about her grandmother being in a "relationship." It was entertaining to watch Leo try so hard to get her attention, but she wasn't sure she was ready for the idea of Bertie dating. If it happened, she would do her best to adapt since she wanted to see her grandmother happy.

Cornelia took a handful of silverware from the dishwasher and spread it out on a towel so each piece could be checked for water spots. "Do you happen to have any magazines in your room?"

Jillian looked at her in surprise. "I have a few."

"I need the tear-out cards from them," Cornelia said. "I collected some at the Clip & Curl but I need more."

"Tear-out cards? Like the subscription cards?" Jillian asked, completely confused.

"Yes."

"Any magazines I have are on the stand next to my bed, but you might want to check the recycling bin in the laundry room. I'm pretty sure Bertie put some in there."

"Good idea."

Jillian almost asked why her aunt wanted tear-out cards, but somehow she wasn't quite sure she wanted to know, so she turned back to take the last few clean dishes from the dishwasher. Once the chore was done, Cornelia excused herself and wandered off in search of magazines. Jillian carried the clean, dry mugs and dishes to the craft services table and filled a few bowls with small bags of chips and granola bars.

After putting out the packaged snacks she whipped up some no-bake cookies since she knew the cast loved sweet treats. No-bake cookies were one of the few things she'd been able to make since she was a teenager whenever she needed a sugar fix. Of course, it helped that they didn't go into the oven. That's when most of Jillian's baking disasters happened. Then again, those disasters weren't happening nearly as often as when she first returned to Moss Hollow.

Once the no-bake cookies were finished, Jillian set to work on the fruit salad so it could soak up the sweet orange dressing before dinnertime. She found the combination of the appealing scent of fresh fruit and the act of chopping helped work out some of the stress from the day she'd had and her worry over Gloria.

She was nearly done when Bibi Bleu walked in. "Have you seen Christopher?"

Jillian shook her head as she pulled the box of plastic wrap from the kitchen drawer. "With shooting suspended for the day, he might be up in his room or maybe hanging out in the living room. How is Ms. Baxter?"

Bibi shook her head morosely. "She has a concussion. The doctor said she won't be able to work for at least three days. She can leave the hospital tomorrow, but she must rest and stay out of the heat."

Jillian doubted the director would be happy to hear that news. "Did she say anything else about what made her fall?"

"I imagine she tripped on something, though it was awfully hot. She might have fainted. She shouldn't have been outside wandering around. She knows the heat is bad for her. It took me forever to find her." She sighed deeply. "Sometimes it's a challenge to be her assistant. I'll go let Christopher know."

Jillian stretched a sheet of plastic over the salad. "Good luck with that."

Bibi winced. "I hope he doesn't decide to kill the messenger." Then she eyed Jillian hopefully. "Would you come with me?"

"Me?" Jillian yelped. "It's a little outside my job description."

"You won't have to say anything," Bibi said. "Just be moral support while he yells at me."

Jillian didn't like the sound of that, but she couldn't resist the other woman's pleading expression. "Sure. Let me just pop this in the fridge."

They headed upstairs after finding the living room contained only Kane Porter, who sat with his feet propped on the coffee table, playing games on his phone. After a single pointed look from Jillian, he took his feet off the table, mumbling a sheepish apology in the process.

Though the upstairs was noticeably warmer than the lower floor, it was still not unpleasant, especially when compared with outside. Bibi walked slower and slower as she got closer to the director's room. Finally she stood directly in front of the door without moving.

"You could be panicking over nothing," Jillian whispered. "He might not be in there."

Bibi forced a smile. "Right." She raised her hand and tapped on the door so softly it barely made a sound. Since Belle Haven had sturdy antique doors, Jillian doubted the sound carried into the room. She gently reached around the assistant and rapped on the door.

Bibi stepped back, nearly treading on Jillian's toes when the door opened and the director stood facing them with a script in his hand. His expression of mild irritation vanished when he saw Bibi. "How is Gloria?"

Bibi gave him the bad news and then shrank back even further, this time actually bumping into Jillian. "Ms. Baxter feels terrible about this, of course."

Christopher slumped, leaning heavily against the door. "We can't afford to lose a couple days of filming. This could sink us, especially if the backers hear about it. They're twitchy enough about the delays we've had."

"Surely, it's not that bad," Bibi said. "Maybe you could film around her."

The director shook his head, a slow defeated movement. "We've been shooting around her too much already, because she didn't want to be out in the heat. The scenes left have to have her in them. We could move up the filming in town if we can get permits in a hurry for the change. Gloria doesn't have any lines in the town scenes, but we definitely see her. We'd still need a stand-in for her." He groaned from frustration then his gaze turned down the hall slightly. "I would have hired a stand-in to begin with if I'd known the misery Gloria was going to put me through." Suddenly his gaze shifted to somewhere behind Jillian and Bibi.

Jillian turned to look. Cornelia was walking toward her room, her arms full of magazines. She must have gotten some of them from the library because her dress was now dusty along with being limp from her earlier walk around the garden. Dust had even settled into her blond hair. Jillian wondered exactly where the magazines had been stored for them to be so dusty.

"Hey," the director called. "Hey, Mrs. Harper."

Cornelia turned, her gaze mildly disapproving. "I'm Mrs. Montgomery. Mrs. Harper is my sister. We may be twins, but I can't believe it's that hard to tell us apart."

"No, of course not," the director said, as he passed Bibi and Jillian. "Mrs. Montgomery, I do believe you're about the same size as Gloria Baxter."

"I imagine so," Cornelia agreed. "The women in my family have always been fine-boned and slender."

"Right," he said absently, walking around Cornelia and looking her up and down.

"Young man," Cornelia snapped, "in the South, men do not stare at women in that manner."

"What do you want with my aunt?" Jillian asked.

The director glanced at her, then back at Cornelia. "With the right costume and makeup, I think she could stand in for Gloria for several of the scenes we need to film. We could add Gloria's voice in post and not lose any more days."

A smile bloomed on Cornelia's face. "You want me to be in the movie?"

"I *need* you to be in the movie."

"My dear husband always said I was quite dramatic."

"You won't actually have to do much acting," the director said. "And your voice won't be in the final cuts, but if you're open to it, we can start tomorrow. I'll have some papers for you to sign."

"I'm not sure Ms. Baxter will like this," Bibi said fretfully.

"Then don't tell her. In fact, don't tell anyone. I can't have loose lips spilling more bad news where my backers can hear it. Have you told anyone about how many days she's going to miss?"

Bibi shook her head. "Just Miss Green and you." Her lips twitched into what might have been a smile on anyone less high strung. "And you told Mrs. Montgomery just now."

"Don't worry about what I've done, worry about what you do. If you want your boss to stay on this project, then I don't want a whisper of this getting out. As far as anyone outside this group knows, I'm expecting Gloria to be out of the hospital and back to filming in town tomorrow. Do you hear?"

"Won't they notice when Gloria doesn't show up?" Jillian asked.

The director snorted. "She's been not showing up for days, so it'll just seem like more of the same. But as far as anyone knows, we're expecting her to be back on the job for shooting in town tomorrow."

"But that will make her sound unprofessional when she can't be there," Bibi protested.

"Being out of work is unprofessional too," he snapped. "She should appreciate the fact that she still has a job."

"Won't people notice that it's Aunt Cornelia on the set instead of Gloria?" Jillian asked.

He shook his head. "It's normal for the major stars to have stand-ins. She would have already had one on *Deadly Gothic* if we weren't working on such a shoestring budget. That bit of cost cutting has bit me enough that no one will be surprised that I did something about it."

Bibi looked from face to face, in clear distress. "This doesn't seem right."

The director flapped a hand at her. "It'll be fine. You keep your lip zipped, and we'll keep making a movie. Now I have to make about a million phone calls." He turned toward Bibi. "You probably have some free time on your hands. Why don't you give me a hand with a few small tasks?"

Her expression reminded Jillian of nature documentaries when prey animals saw predators bearing down on them. Since she didn't vocalize dissent, Christopher towed her into his room, listing the small tasks that didn't sound small at all.

Once the hallway was clear, Cornelia turned toward Jillian, glowing with excitement. "I'm going to be a movie star!"

Jillian managed to smile back, but she had an uneasy feeling that the horror movie was about to turn into a disaster.

6

Cornelia's big debut was to begin at dawn the next morning, so Jillian had to be up early to have breakfast for the cast members who were staying at Belle Haven. Then she had to pack up to drive to town so she could set up the craft services table for the day's shooting. Bertie came down to help start breakfast. She would need to leave early to open the bakery for all the people who would flock to Main Street to watch a real movie being made. She had greeted the news of her sister's impending stardom with horror.

Though Bertie's attitude echoed Jillian's thoughts, she'd been as supportive of Cornelia as she could. It got harder when Cornelia swept downstairs in an outfit that looked more at home at a Halloween party than a breakfast table. The calf-length dress was black chiffon with a tattered hem and butterfly sleeves. The plunging neckline was far deeper than Jillian was comfortable seeing on her aunt.

"Where did you get that outfit?" Jillian asked as soon as she overcame the shock enough to speak.

"It was just something in my closet."

Bertie froze in the act of pulling biscuits from the oven. She groaned and quickly confirmed Jillian's observation. "She wore that last year to the Moss Holloween dance. Where's your pointed hat, Cornelia?"

Her sister sniffed. "I'm finding my character's essence, and the hat doesn't work. Plus, I threw it away when Possum coughed a hairball into the hatbox."

Jillian wrinkled her nose. "Good call."

The costume and makeup department for the movie consisted of Bea, a harried-looking woman of about Jillian's age who tended to wear her glasses perched on top of her head, and Gina, her young assistant who looked so much like her that it was no surprise to learn they were mother and daughter. Gina hurried into the kitchen, looking from Cornelia to Bertie. "Which of you is going to be Ms. Baxter's stand-in?"

Bertie snorted. "The one in a costume."

The young woman looked Cornelia over. "Christopher was right. You look like you'll fit Gloria's wardrobe, but you'll need a wig and a lot of makeup."

Cornelia looked at the woman dubiously. "I have rather delicate skin. How much makeup are we talking about?"

"A lot." She turned to look at Jillian and Bertie. "Mom says we need an air-conditioned spot to do the makeup. This kind of heat and humidity makes the actors sweat too much during application. Christopher told us we could set up in your bakery."

Bertie slammed the sheet of biscuits down on the counter, making them hop. "He did? My bakery is a place of business, not a dressing room."

"Don't be so uptight," Cornelia scolded. "You need to go with the flow."

Jillian stared at her aunt. *Go with the flow?* She had to stifle a snicker when she saw the look Bertie shot toward Cornelia. Jillian knew better than to get between the sisters when her grandmother was wearing that face. She simply turned back to her job of tending bacon on the electric griddle.

"You'll have to work that out with Christopher," Gina said after flicking an amused glance toward Cornelia. "I'm just here to pick up wardrobe for the shoot and head to town." She looked toward the pan of biscuits. "I don't suppose I could have one of those? They look wonderful."

"Sure," Bertie said, though her voice was still tight with irritation. "There's plenty. Jillian, give her some bacon to put on it."

The young woman's eyes lit up as Jillian tucked some of the applewood-smoked bacon into the warm biscuit. She practically snatched it from Jillian's hand, sang out her thanks, then spun on her heel and left. The full wardrobe for *Deadly Gothic* was presently stored in Jillian's home office off of the foyer. Since her office tended to be where they shoved any extra furniture anyway, she figured it might as well function as storage.

The makeup assistant's arrival seemed to be the signal for their houseguests to come clattering downstairs for breakfast. The dark circles under Bibi's eyes made her look exhausted, but everyone else seemed to have taken Gloria's accident in stride. Annika and Kane piled up plates with bacon, biscuits, and fluffy eggs, then carried them to a table in the breakfast nook.

"So much for the myth that actors don't eat," Bertie said.

Leo Shone paused in buttering a biscuit. "Annika and Kane are young. They can eat like locusts and burn it off."

Bertie looked over his filled plate. "And you?"

He grinned and shrugged. "I'm old. No one cares about my physique." He patted his flat stomach and winked at Bertie before carrying his plate to join the other actors.

"That man is a terrible flirt," Bertie complained.

"And you like it," her sister said as she slathered her own biscuits with some of the locally made peach and orange marmalade that Jillian had picked up at the farmer's market.

Bertie harrumphed and gave Christopher Dark a sharp look as he ambled up to fill a plate. "What's this I hear about you using my bakery for makeup?"

"I've been inside it. You have a good space, plus air-conditioning. It seemed the best choice since you are already a vendor for this production." He looked at her steadily, clearly unintimidated by her glare or the way she bristled at the word "vendor." "I'll pay extra, if necessary. I was hoping to wait for a break in the heat to do our in-town shoots, but Gloria's injury has forced a change. Think of how popular your bakery will be during the shooting. Everyone will want to come in and see the makeup department work. We only need a corner and a place to store the day's wardrobe."

"Wardrobe could set up in the side entry," Jillian suggested. "We have a good bit of unused space at the base of the stairs leading to Lenora's apartment, which should offer some privacy since no one comes in that way or goes up the stairs during the day. And if you let the makeup artist set up in the front window, it probably would draw people in. You know how curious folks are in Moss Hollow."

Bertie narrowed her eyes, clearly thinking about it. "I suppose. But if your people get in the way, I'm throwing them out."

As it turned out, Bertie didn't throw the film crew out of the bakery, but she did retreat to the back so she didn't have to watch them work on Cornelia, who clearly had gone Hollywood. She had even forced an autograph on Maggie, who was too polite to refuse.

Jillian watched with amusement for a while, then slipped back into the kitchen to collect the baked goods for the craft services table. Bertie pointed at her. "The crew's food table isn't going in my customer area too, is it?" From the tone of her voice, Jillian was glad that the answer was no.

"Josi volunteered the front reading area in the library. They don't get a lot of people using that space right now because of the heat when the sun comes through the front windows, so she moved the comfy chairs into the back. The front window is a warm spot, but it's still cooler than the street, so it should work and will let anyone eating watch what's going on outside."

"I can't believe a librarian would want people clomping in and out all day," Bertie muttered.

"I think that's the point of libraries," Jillian said, "having people in and out all day."

Bertie harrumphed. "You know none of those movie people care about books. If they did, they wouldn't have their phones in their hands all the time."

"Josi likes people," Lenora said as she began loading mixed pastries into boxes for Jillian. "She'll enjoy all the hubbub. The library is too quiet most of the time. You know the Sweetie Pies ought to do an event to pull more people into the library." The Southern Sweetie Pies were the local baking club who often came together to help out at local fund-raisers and sometimes to gossip shamelessly. Jillian had become an honorary Sweetie Pie as soon as she moved back to Moss Hollow, despite her then-questionable baking skills.

"You ought to bring that up at the next meeting," Jillian said. "I'll add my yes vote. I love the library."

"The Moss Hollow library has a great collection, and folks ought to be reading more." Lenora shook her head. "And to think that just a few generations ago reading was something special that not everyone got to do."

"You're preaching to the choir," Jillian said as she taped the boxes closed and loaded them onto one of the bakery's rolling carts. She turned her attention back to her grandmother. "You know, I thought you'd be cheerier today. I noticed we didn't have any protesters when I drove over."

"It's probably too much to hope they don't come back," Bertie grumbled.

Jillian began pushing the cart toward the door. "We can always hope."

Since the library was just a short way down the street and the sidewalk was level, Jillian figured it would be considerably easier to roll the goods than carry them.

When she got down to the library, she found Josi had already set up some of the library tables and had the library's old percolator on one end of the table, making coffee. "I picked up some flavored creamers too," she said. "It's almost like having some of those fancy doughnut-shop coffees."

"You're a gem," Jillian said. "Give me the receipt for those creamers, and I'll pay you back."

"Oh, I thought if there were any left over, I could keep them for the library." Josi's face pinked slightly. "I like fancy coffee."

"You can still keep any leftovers, but you don't need to pay for the film's coffee out of your pocket," Jillian assured her.

Josi seemed content with that, and she joined Jillian in unloading the boxes of pastries onto the table. Within minutes, they were surrounded by young crew members who had been milling around outside until they saw the tables filling. As always, they praised the goodies with full mouths and even managed a few positive remarks about the coffee.

"Do you know when the filming begins?" Jillian asked one of the young men. She was pretty sure he was a cameraman.

The young man pulled out a cell phone to check the time. "We're due on set in ten minutes."

"Where's the set?" Jillian asked.

He pointed out the window. "Christopher is having a couple blocks of this street closed off."

Jillian looked out the window at the sunny street. The shop

fronts were cheerfully bright and inviting. "It doesn't look very horror movie-esque out there."

"I think that's the point," the young man said, talking around a mouthful of fruit-filled croissant. "The scenes we're shooting today are when Annika and Kane's characters first arrive in town. Anyway, they discover that the town looks great, but all the townsfolk act strange and almost zombie-like. Well, except for Mother Penn. She's just mean. All the extras play the shuffling townsfolk."

Jillian nodded. She had heard that the movie intended to hire dozens of local residents as extras. She'd been so busy that she didn't know if anyone she knew would be among them.

The hungry crew thinned out quickly as the time approached for the filming. Jillian looked over the decimated table, wondering if Leo was right and this was what it felt like to survive a locust swarm. With a sigh, she began cleaning up so she could replace the breakfast offerings with the snack goods that would keep anyone from starving before lunchtime. When she had the tables full, she looked out the window, wondering how her aunt was doing in her new adventure.

Jillian spotted a face she knew well outside the library, and it wasn't Cornelia's. She hurried through the doors, out to the sidewalk and tapped her best friend on the arm. Savannah's face lit up when she saw Jillian. "Are you an extra today too?"

Jillian shook her head. "No, the bakery has to provide food service on location, not just when they're filming at Belle Haven. But I'm surprised to see you here. Weren't you the queen of stage fright in school?"

"And I would be now, but I don't have to say anything. I just have to walk down the street and ignore the cameras and the actors. It'll be fun, and I thought I might have another chance to get Gloria Baxter to sign an autograph."

Before Jillian could give her the bad news about Gloria not being there, she heard a shout behind her. "Hey!" Jillian turned to see a stout man huffing toward her. She vaguely remembered him from one of the first days of filming at the house. He'd complimented Bertie's croissants. "Did you sign the papers?"

"Me?" Jillian yelped. "Papers for what?"

The man rolled his eyes. "For being an extra. No one appears on camera until they sign the papers."

"I don't want to be an extra," Jillian said. "I'm doing craft services. I just came out here to say hi to my friend."

The man smirked at her. "How sweet. Now go on inside and watch the chips and dip so you don't end up on camera."

Annoyed by the man's tone, Jillian wrestled with the urge to root in place just because she didn't like being ordered around. From the corner of her eye, she caught Savannah's amused look. Clearly her friend was waiting for the fireworks. Jillian had enough of her grandmother in her that smart people didn't get too snarky with her.

"Jillian! Jillian, look at me!" Jillian looked up to see her aunt waving from the opposite sidewalk. It was the first time Jillian had seen her aunt since the makeup artist had finished with her. The transformation was striking. Cornelia's face looked far more gaunt than usual, and the dark, dowdy dress she wore was the exact opposite of the pastel florals her aunt usually chose. Plus, the wig was a perfect copy of Gloria's tight chignon. But Jillian doubted Gloria's character ever waved and fluttered quite like Cornelia Montgomery.

The man moaned. "It's like herding cats around here." He strode into the street. "You need to get back to your mark!"

Cornelia looked around at the empty sidewalk.

"Not a literal mark, the place I told you to stand!"

His snotty tone sent a sense of annoyance up Jillian's spine.

She took a few steps toward the edge of the sidewalk, intending to cross the street and give that obnoxious man a piece of her mind. She didn't like hearing anyone speak disrespectfully to her aunt.

The man reached Cornelia and grabbed her arm, towing her back toward her imaginary mark. Cornelia wrenched her arm free, stumbling backward a few steps just as someone screamed, the pitch high. "Savannah?"

In the instant before Jillian could turn to look at her friend, she saw what made Savannah scream. A huge light fixture, surely something from the film crew, pelted down from the roof of the building directly toward Cornelia below.

Yelling, Jillian raced across the street with Savannah right behind her as the huge light hit the pavement. For a heart-stopping moment, Jillian wasn't sure if it had struck her aunt, as neither she nor the crewman was standing. Then she realized Cornelia was crouched beside the howling man who had his hands clasped to his leg.

"Are you all right?" Jillian asked Cornelia.

"I'm fine," Cornelia said, half-yelling to be heard over the man's howling. "But when that thing hit the sidewalk, a piece bounced back into his leg. He pulled it out." She looked down at the man and shouted. "You should never pull something like that out."

Jillian wasn't sure the man appreciated the lecture, though it was hard to tell through the screaming. She knelt beside him and saw the wound was bleeding profusely, but not in spurts. She knew spurts were bad. She pulled off her crisp, white bakery apron and pressed it against the wound as she looked back at Savannah. "Call 911."

"I already called." Sheriff's Deputy Laura Lee Zane slipped in beside Jillian and clamped her hands to the apron. She looked up at Jillian, speaking in her efficient, no-nonsense tone. "They're on their way and one of the other deputies ran for the first aid kit. I can get this. If Cornelia is all right, you should find her a place to sit down." Then Laura turned to Savannah. "More help is coming, but we're getting a crowd. Can you help keep them back?"

Jillian stood up, her nerves calmed by Laura Lee's crisp efficiency. The first time Jillian met Laura Lee, the deputy had seemed so young, but Jillian had quickly learned the young woman was also intelligent and fearless. She had become one of Jillian's best friends in Moss Hollow.

She felt moisture against her shin and looked down to see blood had soaked into the lower leg of her white slacks. She shuddered at the feeling.

With the apron clamped to his wound, the man finally stopped howling, and was simply moaning quietly. He looked pale and shaky. Jillian moved away to give Laura Lee more room as Savannah turned toward the swiftly gathering crowd. "Stay back," she shouted. "Give the deputy room to work."

The crowd barely shuffled backward, and they all jostled for the best view of the wreckage and the bleeding man. Savannah continued to herd them with calm, firm directions.

Since Savannah clearly had the crowd under control and Jillian figured more deputies would be along for crowd control, she caught Cornelia by the arm and led her away from the fray. "Are you sure you're all right?"

Cornelia nodded. Her wig was slightly askew, revealing a peek of blonde curls at her temple. "You'll need some time with wardrobe," Jillian said lightly, concerned at her aunt's pale silence.

"I doubt it."

"Why?"

Cornelia turned to look at Jillian, her expression eerily calm. "I finally see it. I can't believe I didn't realize earlier."

"See what?"

"The dead bird was a message from the haint, a warning, and I didn't pay any attention. I've been so foolish."

Jillian shook Cornelia's arm gently, trying to snap her aunt out of her odd, flat calmness. "The bird had nothing to do with the haint, and this was just some kind of accident."

Cornelia managed a weak, pitying smile at that. "Don't be silly, Jillian. The movie is cursed. It happens all the time." She shook her head in slow sweeps. "I should never have let them come to Belle Haven. Who knows what the curse will do next?"

Jillian groaned. "There's no curse, Cornelia. The movie has had some accidents, yes. They're probably the result of trying to do too much with not enough crew or funding or safety measures, but they have nothing to do with a curse."

Cornelia patted Jillian's arm. "I'm going over to the bakery for a cup of tea and a seat. I don't think we'll be filming anything soon."

"I'll walk with you." Jillian didn't want to leave her aunt alone while she looked pale and was acting so strangely. And she desperately wanted to change her stained slacks for some of the spare clothes she kept in the bakery's storage room.

Heading for the bakery, they had some trouble navigating against the tide of people coming to rubberneck at the accident. Jillian saw two more deputies join the crowd as they made their way out. She was sure they'd soon get things back in order.

The bakery stood nearly empty when they walked in. Only Bea, the makeup artist, and Maggie were in the customer area, and they both stared out the window at the crowd on the sidewalk across the street. "What happened?" Maggie asked as soon as they walked in, obviously eyeing the blood on Jillian's slacks.

"A light fell from the top of that building." Jillian said. Cornelia stopped near the window and stared out. Jillian gave her aunt's arm a small tug, but Cornelia stayed rooted to the spot, so Jillian sighed and explained further about the light. "It hit the sidewalk, but a broken piece hit one of the crew. I think the guy was in charge of the extras."

The makeup artist winced. "That would be Jorge. He's part of casting. I don't like him much, but I hope he's all right."

"I think he will be," Jillian assured her. "The deputy is helping him." She turned toward her aunt. "I thought you wanted some tea."

Cornelia patted Jillian's arm without looking at her. "That's a good idea. Get me some, please. I'll wait here."

"Maybe you should sit down."

"I'm fine here." Cornelia finally turned to look directly at her. "My tea?"

Jillian headed behind the counter where they had a large coffeemaker that had a small spigot for hot water. She filled the mug she normally used for her own morning coffee at the bakery—Cornelia didn't like foam cups for tea. Jillian rummaged for a tea bag of Cornelia's favorite peach flavor, making a mental note that they needed to order more. As she dunked the bag up and down in the hot water, Bertie bustled out of the kitchen with a pan of brownies. She stopped and looked around the empty room. "Where are all my customers?"

"They went outside to look at the accident," Maggie yelled over to her.

"Accident?" Bertie echoed.

While she continued to slosh the tea bag, Jillian explained about the falling light.

"Sounds like those people aren't paying proper attention," Bertie grumbled. "Are you all right, Cornelia?"

"Of course, but the movie will have to be stopped."

Bertie looked confused. "Why is that?"

"Because it's cursed." Cornelia had drifted over to the counter and picked up a brownie. Jillian rolled her eyes at her aunt and set her mug of tea on the counter.

"Those are for customers," Bertie chastised Cornelia as she took a bite of the brownie, "and what on earth are you talking about?"

"I really shouldn't have taken so long to realize what's going on. The movie is cursed." Then her eyes widened. "Or it may just be the role of Mother Penn that is cursed. Gloria had it and she ended up in the hospital, then I get it and a light almost smashed me. Though either way, they really should stop filming. I don't see any other solution, as much as I hate giving up my debut."

"You don't have a role," Bertie said. "You're a stand-in. You're basically a placeholder until Gloria gets back."

Cornelia made a face at her sister. "Every star starts somewhere." Then she took another bite of her brownie.

"You're a little old to be planning your movie career," Bertie snarked. "But your stardom isn't the point. The movie isn't cursed. Gloria just fell down because she was wandering around where she shouldn't have been and she tripped. And the light fell because it wasn't properly anchored." She turned and looked pointedly at Jillian. "Why are you so quiet? You're usually quick to pooh-pooh all of Cornelia's haint mumbo jumbo."

"I'm sure the movie isn't cursed. I already told Aunt Cornelia that," Jillian said, speaking quietly so her words wouldn't carry to Maggie and the makeup artist at the window. "But Gloria did say she thought someone was trying to kill her. What if something more human is at play here?"

Bertie harrumphed. "Don't go looking for mysteries where they don't exist. Gloria was probably looking for publicity so she made up something dramatic."

"Then why whisper it privately to me?" Jillian asked. "Why not yell it all the way to the ambulance?"

"I don't know, for sure," her grandmother admitted, "but I doubt we have anything more happening here than bad safety measures. You wait, you'll start hearing Gloria's theory all over the set once she has a chance to whisper it to a few more people. Nothing spreads better than a secret." Her grandmother pointed a sharp finger at Jillian's pant leg. "And change your pants. No one will want to eat food served by someone in bloody clothes."

"I'm not sure that would actually slow down this crew," Jillian said, but since she was desperate to change, she followed her grandmother's order, walking briskly through the hot kitchen to the storeroom and pulling on a clean pair of white slacks. She found an empty bucket, filled it with cold water at the storage room sink, and left her stained pants soaking.

She returned to the front of the bakery in time to find everyone still looking out the window, except Bertie, who was very pointedly wiping the tops of display counters instead of paying attention to the melee outside.

"There's Christopher!" Bea said. "I'm going out there." She looked back toward Bertie on her way to the door. "Don't let anyone mess with my makeup."

"I'm running a business here," Bertie said, but the woman paid no attention to her and walked out. With the door open, Jillian could hear the director shouting to the crowd. She walked over to stand in the doorway, and Cornelia trailed after her.

"As soon as the ambulance leaves with Jorge, I want this mess cleared away," the director bellowed at the crowd of crew and extras milling around the street. "We can still film the town scenes as long as we get done before nightfall. We've got plenty of daylight."

"I'm not paying to air-condition all of Moss Hollow," Bertie yelled from behind the counter. "If you and Cornelia need to listen to that man, go on. But stay out of trouble."

Cornelia made a face at her sister, but then walked outside with her tea mug still in hand, and Jillian followed her. Jillian was interested in why Gooder Jones was standing almost nose-to-nose with the director and wondered when he'd arrived. She looked around for Laura Lee but couldn't spot the younger deputy in the crowd of bystanders. "You are not to clear away the debris until I finish my investigation."

"What investigation?" The director stood with his hands on his hips, leaning toward the slightly shorter deputy. If it weren't for the feather-shedding vest, he might have been an intimidating figure, dressed all in black with a fierce scowl. "The light fell. It was an accident and heads will roll, but we need to get back to work."

"That light could have killed someone," Gooder said. "And this is not the first time an ambulance has been called to your film set. So I'm going to look closely at what made the light fall, and if I don't like what I see, you're going to have some trouble."

"A threat," the director roared. "This officer threatened me." He pointed to a nervous young woman trailing along behind him. "Get my lawyer on the phone. This man threatened me."

The woman fumbled her cell phone out of her pocket, nearly dropping it in her haste. She held the phone close to her nose as if she needed glasses and tapped at the screen. Neither the director nor the deputy paid any attention to her.

"It's the middle of the day in the Georgia summer," Gooder said. "Why did you need a big light on the building anyway?"

Christopher Dark looked uncomfortable for the first time. He looked up toward the roofline of the buildings. "I don't actually know," he admitted. "I had the crew bring the big lights in case we ended up filming late on the street, but I expected them to stay on the truck." He shrugged. "I'm sure someone was just trying to be proactive in case we worked late."

"Who?" Gooder asked. "Who would have put it up there?"

The director turned back to the crowd and demanded to know who had put the light on the building. Though the crowd rustled and buzzed with conversation, no one stepped forward.

The young woman with the phone stepped up behind the director and tapped him on the arm, making him jump. "What?" he shouted at her.

She held out the phone. "It's your lawyer."

The director looked at her blankly. "What's he want?"

The woman's expression turned panicky. "You called him."

"No I didn't," the director snapped, thrusting the phone back at her. "This isn't even my phone." He turned back to Gooder, who seemed to be struggling to suppress a smile. "Fine, do your investigation and we'll take a break, but I want to be filming again after lunch."

"I'll be done when I'm done," Gooder said, stretching his usual Southern drawl out like warm honey.

The director glared at him for a moment, then spun and stomped away so quickly he nearly ran over the young woman chirping apologetically into her phone. Gooder strolled over to Jillian. "That man is an idiot."

"I think he's probably a little stressed," Jillian said. "Accidents cost money, and I get the feeling this production is being done on a shoestring that is stretched to the breaking point. I'm surprised to see you. I saw Laura Lee here earlier."

Gooder groaned. "She's working crowd control, which is why she was here first. But unfortunately this is my case because I came out to your place yesterday." He frowned. "And speaking of your place, I'm surprised I haven't seen those nutty protesters. Didn't they get the memo that you were going to be in town today?"

"I don't know," Jillian said. "I thought maybe you scared them off. They weren't in the driveway this morning."

Gooder lifted his eyebrows. "Interesting. I think I'll look into where they might have been earlier when the light incident happened."

"I couldn't really picture that group of women hauling that heavy light up the outside stairs to the roof of that building. I've seen those steps. They're iron and they're steep. It couldn't have been a quiet process."

"And yet, somehow no one knows anything."

"Or isn't saying. I know Christopher Dark doesn't want anything said that might upset the investors in the movie."

"You know, money problems could explain the accidents," Gooder said. "I think I'll see what I can track down about the movie's finances."

"I'd love to hear what you find out," Jillian said.

Gooder smirked at her. "I'm sure you would, but try not to hold your breath too long waiting. We've been filling up the hospital enough lately."

Jillian crossed her arms over her chest and gave Gooder her best glare. "Have you talked to Gloria about her accident?"

He nodded. "Briefly. She insists someone is trying to kill her, but since she wasn't here at all today, it seems to undermine that theory."

"Unless they mistook me for Gloria," Cornelia said. She had slipped up on them quietly during the conversation.

Gooder looked her over. "Surely everyone knew Gloria wasn't going to be here."

"Actually, they didn't," Jillian said. "The director insisted we act as if we expected Gloria to be here. He doesn't want his backers to find out *Deadly Gothic* is in trouble."

Gooder groaned. "Great, so I can thin the suspect list down to everyone in Moss Hollow today. Surely it would have to have been a crew member who got to the light and put it on the building."

"Maybe," Jillian said. "It would certainly draw less attention if it were crew, but there's virtually no security, and there are so many people here today. This kind of crowd could hide a lot."

Gooder's scowl darkened. "I'm going to hope this turns out to be a string of unfortunate coincidences, because the last thing I need is some nut dropping things out of the sky on purpose."

He stomped away down the street, and Jillian turned to her aunt. "I was surprised to hear you say someone might have mistaken you for Gloria. I thought you were going for the movie curse explanation."

"They aren't mutually exclusive," Cornelia said, "but I don't wish to be accidentally murdered. I look forward to the day I can rejoin my darling Raymond, but I have no desire to hasten it along."

"And a curse sounds more comforting to you?"

Cornelia smiled. "Of course, dear. I have friends in the spirit realm who could help me with a curse. My dearest Raymond would never let something like that harm me." Her gaze turned toward the roofline. "Perhaps that's why the light didn't hit me today. Maybe Raymond deflected it."

Somehow Jillian doubted that her sweet-natured great-uncle had turned into Superman in his afterlife, but she was glad to see Cornelia seemed less shaken than she had earlier. "Well, whether we're experiencing accidents, curses, or a murder attempt, we should all be very careful while this film crew is here."

Cornelia smiled over the edge of her tea mug. "I'm always careful, dear. You're the one who takes wild chances. Perhaps I should be warning you." She turned toward the milling crowd and spoke more loudly. "In fact, it's possible I should be warning everyone."

The closest of the crowd turned to look in her direction. One of the beefy guys who had hauled around most of the heavy equipment for the movie looked at Cornelia suspiciously. "Warn us about what?"

"It's entirely possible this movie is cursed," Cornelia answered, her voice especially loud on the last word.

The word "curse" buzzed through the crowd like an electric current, and Jillian groaned, certain that her aunt's kooky theory could only make things worse. *If there is such a thing as a self-fulfilling prophecy, Aunt Cornelia has added a few dozen acolytes to hasten the prophecy along.*

8

With the filming postponed, the crew members not involved in the cleanup descended on the library, looking for snacks. Savannah came in to help Jillian keep the tables filled with brownie bites, bags of chips, granola bars, and fresh fruit. As Jillian watched the crew work its way through all the snacks she'd brought for morning and afternoon, she began to agree with Leo. These people *were* human locusts.

Finally she had to close the table to switch over to lunch. "Can you help Lenora and Bertie set up the lunch trays?" she asked Savannah. "I'm going to have to run to the grocery store and get snacks for the afternoon. Our contract says food has to be available throughout the workday."

"No problem," Savannah said cheerily. "Is Cornelia going to help? I'm surprised I don't see her."

"I had Josi take her to the break room," Jillian said. "I wanted to cut down on the curse talk around the crew, and I thought Cornelia looked a little worn out. I think almost getting killed is starting to sink in."

"Well, if anyone can take good care of Cornelia, it's Josi," Savannah said. "She's a sweetheart."

With most of Moss Hollow's attention on the horror-movie filming, Jillian found the grocery practically empty and surprisingly restful. With narrow aisles and fluorescent lights that were prone to flicker and buzz, the little store was a far cry from the big supermarkets Jillian had frequented in California. Still, Food for Less stocked local produce, and the manager was always open to ordering any "weird Yankee food" that Jillian might want, so she had become quite fond of it. Like everything in Moss Hollow, it was a little quirky, but felt like home. She stood in the chip aisle with two bags of organic tortilla chips in her hands, debating between them when a deep voice spoke behind her. "You must be stocking up for quite a party."

Jillian turned to see Hunter Greyson holding a carton of half-and-half and a small bag of sugar. He looked handsome as always in a crisp, well-tailored suit. She couldn't understand how anyone could wear a suit in the middle of Georgia summer and not look like limp lettuce, but somehow Hunter managed. She wondered if it was part of his genetic makeup since he came from a long line of morticians. As the disjointed thoughts tumbled through her head, she stared blankly at him a bit longer than she should have.

Hunter waved a hand in front of her face. "Hello? Earth to Jillian."

"Oh, sorry. I'm a little tired." She turned and tossed both bags into her cart. "It's been a stressful week. You know we've had a film crew out at Belle Haven?"

He nodded. "I'd heard. In fact, the location scout wanted to do some filming in Greyson & Sons, but I don't think that's the sort of publicity we're looking for."

"Smart man. I'm beginning to wish I'd shown that kind of smarts."

"Oh?"

"I'd be glad to tell you, but can we shop and chat? I need to be back to set up the afternoon craft services table."

"Of course."

Hunter fell into step beside her, and Jillian caught him up on the events of the last few days while grabbing stray snack items from the shelves. "So now the accidents are piling up, and I still don't know how a dead crow got into Belle Haven, and I'm beginning to seriously worry about Aunt Cornelia's safety. Plus, I'm not looking forward to the return of our own personal protesters."

"Have you spoken with the police?"

Jillian sighed. "I've talked to Gooder Jones, as anything connected to *Deadly Gothic* seems to be officially his case. I will say that he's starting to take it seriously since Aunt Cornelia was nearly smooshed, but I'm not finding him as reassuring as I would like."

Hunter smiled. "And you're wired to ask questions and poke into things until you find answers, a trait that drives him crazy."

Jillian stopped her cart, causing the pile of snacks to wobble precariously. "You make me sound nosy."

"Not nosy, but definitely curious and tenacious. Those aren't bad qualities. I admire them."

She looked at him closely, not sure if he was teasing her. Hunter was something of a mystery himself. He could be so formal one minute, and the next, he'd be rolling up his sleeves and helping out on some project or other, grinning the whole time. Finally she began pushing her cart toward the registers again. "I just wish I knew what I ought to do next."

"First, I would appreciate it if you tried to be careful. I would be very upset to lose one of the most interesting people in Moss Hollow."

Jillian felt warmth flood her face so she turned to look at one of the near shelves to hide the blush. She picked up a couple boxes of cheesy crackers that she probably didn't need and added them to the overflowing cart. "I didn't know you were such a flatterer," she said, making a point to keep her voice light.

"Just honest. You know, it seems to me that Gloria has a story to tell," Hunter said, catching a bag of chips that tumbled out of Jillian's cart. "Perhaps you should ask her to tell it."

Jillian nodded. *That's a good idea.* "I think you're right. In fact, if I hurry, I might have time to go to the hospital before I head back to set up the table." She gave him a bright smile as she pushed the cart to the nearest register, grabbing up one of the small bouquets from a display along the way. "Thanks for the suggestion."

"Any time. I hope you'll let me know how this turns out. We can have dinner somewhere and you can regale me with Hollywood stories."

"I'm not sure how good they would be."

Hunter chuckled at that. "If there is one thing I'm certain of, it's that Jillian Green *always* has a good story to tell."

"I'll do my best." She held up the bouquet. "I need to head for the hospital."

Hunter pointed at her with his carton of half-and-half. "You will be careful?"

"I promise."

Within minutes, Jillian was checked out and on the way to the Nathan County Hospital. She knew she'd be pushing near the limits of the time available, but she felt more and more that Hunter was right. She needed to hear Gloria's story. The actress believed someone was trying to kill her, or it certainly had sounded like she believed it. Maybe Gloria was basing her belief on more than one push. Maybe she even had an idea who might be angry enough with her to kill her.

Jillian ran her mind through the crew members she'd actually chatted with in the last few days. She assumed she could eliminate the poor man who'd nearly been flattened by the falling light. If he was trying to kill Gloria, he was certainly inept. As she went over the other people, she didn't come up with terribly compelling motives. Christopher Dark was upset with Gloria because she was costing the movie so much money, but that wasn't likely to be improved by killing her. Then the movie would be scrapped altogether.

There was clearly no love lost between Annika and Gloria, but petty sniping didn't seem like a motive to murder someone, and Annika had sounded genuinely confused when Gloria had accused her of leaving the bird in the bathroom. Of course, Jillian was reminded of what Gooder had said. *These people are actors.*

Speaking of actors, she couldn't think of any reason for Kane or Leo to hate Gloria. Gloria wasn't nice to them, but she was no less so than to anyone else. And Jillian felt certain that Kane's concern for the crow was genuine. Plus, Leo's full attention seemed to be on Bertie, not Gloria.

She did wonder about Bibi Bleu. On the surface, the woman appeared to be devoted to Gloria, but the actress certainly treated her horribly. Of course, Gloria seemed to treat everyone horribly. Still, as Gloria's assistant, Bibi was a handy target for daily abuse. Maybe that was enough to make her snap. Then Jillian remembered walking in on Bibi scrubbing her hands in the laundry room sink. *Had she been trying to wash away blood from the crow?* And if Gloria believed Bibi was behind the accidents, it might explain why she talked to Jillian and not Bibi.

Finally, Jillian considered and discarded the protesters. Even though *Deadly Gothic* would certainly be stopped if they had enough accidents, it seemed an extreme plan for a group made up of ordinary women.

The Nathan County Hospital was situated halfway between Moss Hollow and Painter's Ridge, so the drive gave Jillian plenty of time to think. As she turned over the events of the last few days, she barely noticed the lush landscape of moss-draped Live Oaks and beautifully landscaped gardens. Not everyone in Nathan County had money—not by a long shot—but there was a pervasive sense of pride in their homes and their land that tended to be reflected in their lawns and gardens above all else. Jillian often enjoyed driving around just to admire the color and variety of plants, but since this was no pleasure drive, the bulk of her attention was on the past few days, not the beauty around her now.

By the time she pulled into the parking lot at the county hospital, she had herself half-convinced that Bibi Bleu was a potential murderer. At the very least, she was at the top of Jillian's list of persons of interest.

When she walked into the large, brightly lit hospital foyer, Jillian recognized the elderly woman with faintly blue hair and pink volunteer smock, who sat behind the information desk. It was the same woman who'd given her information the first time she'd visited someone in the hospital after coming back to Georgia. As Jillian walked closer, the woman peered at her with a hopeful smile but no sign of recognition. "May I help you?"

"I'm looking for Gloria Baxter's room," Jillian said.

The volunteer's watery blue eyes widened. "The actress? I heard she was here. It's hard to imagine a big star in our little hospital. You know, I saw her first movie ever. She was so beautiful."

Jillian tried to picture the pinch-faced actress as beautiful and found her imagination didn't stretch that far. She made a mental note to track down a copy of *Hexe* sometime and watch it. "I haven't seen that movie."

"Well, you should," the woman said fervently. "It was so scary. Not scary like movies today with their computer monsters and gore, but the kind of scary where your own imagination does half the work. And the movie was cursed, of course, which just made it scarier."

"Cursed?"

"Oh yes, everyone said the movie was cursed. My mama said the curse was just some publicity stunt, but it wasn't a stunt when Annie Venture died."

The name slapped Jillian in the face. Annie Venture. Annika Venn. Surely two names being so similar wasn't a coincidence.

"Do you know what Annie Venture looked like?" Jillian asked softly

"She was a pretty little thing; a lot like Gloria, with the blonde hair and blue eyes. Though you couldn't tell eye color from the movie, of course. It was in black and white, but I used to read the movie magazines." The woman sighed. "Annie always seemed so sweet. According to the movie magazines, she grew up in a small Texas town and moved to Hollywood to become a movie star. *Hexe* was her first starring role."

Jillian stood silent for a moment, wondering how much to make of the similarities. Both movies had actresses with similar-sounding names, and both had actresses who were injured during the filming, though at least Gloria had survived her accident. It certainly felt like the attacks on Gloria must be connected to *Hexe*. The similarities were too coincidental. *Weren't they?*

The volunteer's slightly wobbly voice broke into Jillian's thoughts. "You know her?"

"Excuse me?"

"Gloria Baxter. Do you know her?"

"She's in a movie that is filming at my home, Belle Haven."

"Belle Haven. I know that house." The smile that spread across the woman's face made it suddenly easier for Jillian to imagine this particular elderly woman when she was young. "You must be Bertie's girl."

"Her granddaughter," Jillian said.

"Bertie and Cornelia grew up with my little sister, Martha." The woman sighed. "Martha's gone now. It's sad how that happens sometimes. I never expected to outlive my kid sister." She forced a smile that didn't reach her eyes. "Please, tell Bertie and Cornelia that I said hi."

"I will." Jillian let her eyes drift to the stick-on name tag on the woman's thin chest. "Agnes."

Agnes bobbed her head, her smile shining. "I just need to make sure she's on the list for visitors. If so, I'll get you that room number." She turned to the computer on the desk and poked at it tentatively for a moment before scribbling a number on one of the hospital maps. She marked the route Jillian should take onto the map with highlighter and handed it over. "I hope Gloria gets well soon."

"Me too."

Before Jillian could turn away, the woman reached out to touch her arm. "I was wondering. What's the name of the movie?"

"The one filming at Belle Haven? *Deadly Gothic.*"

The woman smiled, making her eyes nearly vanish in the wrinkles around them. "I'll be sure to see it when it comes out."

If it comes out, Jillian thought, but she only smiled back and wished the woman a good day before following the map through the confusing maze of hospital corridors. Like many hospitals with multiple additions, there were twists and turns that seemed to make no sense at all, but Jillian followed the map carefully and made it to Gloria's wing without getting lost.

She had expected to find the halls around Gloria's room orderly and quiet, but instead she spotted nurses and doctors frantically running and shouting orders. The noise and confusion centered on a single room so Jillian automatically turned toward it. The door to the room hung open, but the crowd around the bed obscured the patient. Jillian listened to the clipped, serious voices. Clearly the person in the bed was in trouble.

Jillian whispered a soft prayer for whoever lay in the bed behind the shifting wall of nurses and doctors. Then her gaze turned again to the paper, checking for Gloria's room number and comparing it to those on the walls. With a gasp, she saw the number on the paper and the room number matched.

The patient dying in the room in front of her was Gloria Baxter.

9

Jillian stepped toward the room. She stood silently with the map clutched in one hand and the small bouquet in the other. How could Gloria be dying? She'd seemed fine, if slightly confused, at Belle Haven. But the bustle in Gloria's room made it plain that Jillian's evaluation was wrong.

A doctor walked out of Gloria's room, his fine brown hair rumpled and his glasses slightly askew. The doctor's skin was so smooth that Jillian had a moment to wonder how old he was. Then she almost smiled. *I must be getting old when doctors look like children.* "Excuse me?" She pointed toward Gloria's room. "What's going on with Gloria?"

He looked at her directly, and Jillian saw him slip into his bedside manner like an invisible suit. "Are you a relative?"

Instead of answering directly, Jillian just stared at the room and whispered, "Is she going to be all right?"

The doctor seemed to take her apparent distress as proof enough of her connection to Gloria. "She coded, but we're doing everything we can."

"Coded?"

"Her heart stopped." He raised a hand before Jillian could speak. "We've gotten it restarted, but it's too early to know her present condition. At the moment, she is in a coma."

"She was fine," Jillian said, her distress now completely unfeigned. "How did her heart just stop?"

The young doctor took a deep breath. "It appears she was given the wrong medication. We're not sure how the notation for the wrong medicine was entered on her chart. I'm her doctor, but

I definitely did not put that on her chart. The hospital will track down this error. In the meanwhile, I promise you, we're doing everything we can for Ms. Baxter."

"Doctor Leighton!"

Both the young doctor and Jillian turned at the sharp voice of a much older man in a white lab coat. He glared at the younger man. "May I speak to you? Now!"

The young doctor's face paled sharply. He turned for a moment to Jillian. "Excuse me." Then he spun on his heel and walked toward the older man. Jillian suspected he was going to be in trouble for being so forthright about the hospital's mistake, but she wondered just how much of this was the hospital's mistake. *Another accident?* It seemed so unlikely. At the same time, if someone did intentionally alter Gloria's chart, who could have done it? And who would even know what medicine to give her to induce a heart attack? Jillian certainly wouldn't have.

Jillian carried her small bouquet of flowers to the nurse's station and handed them to the only person there, a young woman flipping through a clipboard of papers. "Could you give this to one of the patients who doesn't have flowers?"

"Of course." The young woman smiled at Jillian. "That's nice of you."

She turned away from the nurse's station and was surprised to see a flash of burgundy hair as someone ducked quickly into the small chapel at the end of the hall. *I know that color.* Jillian walked to the room and looked in. She saw a woman on her knees with a large tote bag resting on the floor next to her. She had knelt very near a backlit stained glass window at the front of the room; her hair was covered by a white scarf. *Could it be Colette, the leader of the protesters? She could certainly have fit her fancy camera in that bag. If it is her, what's she doing at the hospital? Maybe interfering with someone's chart?*

She took a hesitant step into the chapel. Her idea seemed so far-fetched, and if the woman on her knees wasn't Collette, Jillian would be intruding on someone's prayers. She decided to wait until the woman came out of the room. At that point, she should be able to get a good look at her. Jillian backed out quietly and loitered near the door, feeling more than a little out of place.

"May I help you?" Jillian turned to face a gray-haired man in a clerical collar who gave her a serene smile. "You shouldn't hesitate to go in and pray. Many people find peace in the midst of the storm in that very room. He peeked around the doorway and must have assumed the praying woman was the reason Jillian had not entered. "There is enough space inside for more than one person to pray."

"Oh, no, I mean, yes. I often find peace in prayer, but I wasn't waiting to go into the chapel."

He raised his eyebrows. "Then what were you waiting for?"

"Nothing." She smiled, not knowing how to explain without sounding like a stalker. "Actually I have to leave."

She turned and hurried away, her face burning with embarrassment. She certainly couldn't have told the hospital chaplain that she was hanging around to check out someone praying in the chapel. It probably wasn't Collette anyway. *There are plenty of people who dye their hair strange colors.*

Jillian left the hospital and made the drive back to downtown Moss Hollow with even more on her mind than before, as well as an uncomfortable sense of déjà vu. When she first came back to Moss Hollow, she'd tried to visit someone in that very hospital and the woman had died while Jillian stood in the hall. That death had been murder. Jillian felt sure that Gloria's condition was attempted murder as well. The big question was who was trying to kill the aging actress and why. *Could it be the leader of the protesters? And if so, why?*

Main Street was still closed for the blocks around the movie shoot, so Jillian had to take a back street to reach the alley that led to parking behind the bakery. She hauled her bags of snacks out of her snow-white Prius and headed for the back door of the bakery, heavily loaded down with the cloth grocery bags. Getting the back door open with her arms so full was tricky, but Jillian had carried enough trays of goods in and out that very door to have perfected the use of her feet as door-opening tools.

As she walked through the steaming kitchen, she spotted Lenora pulling golden-brown yeast rolls from one of the ovens and the homey smell made Jillian's stomach growl, reminding her that it was past lunchtime—a lunch that she hadn't eaten.

Lenora grinned, her white, even teeth bright against her dark skin. Lenora Ryan had been working at the bakery for as long as Jillian could remember, and she tended to be a warm pool of sanity in the chaos of Jillian's life. "Well, the gadabout is back," Lenora said. "You best hurry. Those movie people ate every bit of the lunch we made, and I had to have my cousin bring a couple buckets of chicken from Cheap Cheap Chicken so folks didn't turn hostile."

"They were probably bored on the long break. Bored people eat." Jillian held up the stuffed bags. "I have supplies."

"You took long enough getting them," Lenora scolded.

"I ran over to the hospital to check on Gloria Baxter."

Lenora's expression changed instantly. "That poor lady. Is she feeling better?"

Jillian shifted uncomfortably, trying to ease the tension of the bag straps cutting into her wrists. "Unfortunately not. In fact, someone gave her the wrong medicine. She's very sick."

"Whoo-ee, a body would almost side with Cornelia on this. Sounds like that movie *is* cursed."

Jillian heard a groan and turned toward the doorway leading to the customer area of the bakery. Her grandmother stood there with her arms crossed. "Enough with that ridiculous curse talk." She pointed at Jillian. "I set out cheddar puffs and brownies, but you'll need more snacks. Savannah is manning the table. You're lucky to have such amazing friends. Not many people would look after *your* job like that."

"I know. I'm going." Jillian slipped by her grandmother and walked through the customer area. Some of the crew had found their way to the bakery where the selection of treats was more extensive than at the craft services table. Even with free food just down the sidewalk, they were apparently willing to pay for Chocolate Shoppe éclairs and cupcakes. Not that Jillian blamed them.

The transition from the cool customer area to the heat of the sidewalk was almost painful. The sidewalk was crowded with actors and extras all turned toward the street, so Jillian had to inch along with her load, staying close to the buildings.

The afternoon filming would actually be on the opposite sidewalk. Through a tiny break in the crowd, Jillian saw the other side of the street was nearly empty except for the director, and a small group of actors and crew. Christopher was waving his arms in big gestures while talking to Annika and Cornelia. Jillian noticed there was no sign of the fallen light. Apparently Gooder had finally let them clean it up.

She paused for a moment, watching Annika. The young actress leaned slightly toward the director, her attention riveted. Jillian thought again about the similarity of names between Annika Venn and Annie Venture. She knew weird coincidences happened all the time, but they were piling up around *Deadly Gothic*, and Jillian felt they all tied together somehow.

Pulling herself away from watching, Jillian bulldozed through the crowd with her burden of bags and managed to reach the library. Even with so many people on the street, there was still a group milling around the craft services table. Jillian could see the selection of food was becoming sparse indeed. Savannah greeted her with real relief. "I was starting to think I'd need to go through my purse and start passing out mints."

"Sorry." Jillian tore open one of the bags of chips and dumped it into the nearly empty chip bowl. She passed along a box of granola bars for Savannah to put out. "How are we doing on cold drinks?"

"Thankfully, we seem to be doing okay on those," Savannah said as she set out the bars. "What else did you bring?"

Jillian handed her the insulated bag that held a stack of small cheese platters she'd picked up at the grocery's deli. Then she opened a different style of chips and filled another bowl before squatting to root around for the jars of salsa. "I'm sorry to have left you so long. I went by the hospital." She stood and dumped the salsa into a bowl.

She noticed the raised eyebrows and questioning look on Savannah's face so she leaned close and quietly caught her up on what she had learned at the hospital.

"I'm so sorry," Savannah said. "Do they think Gloria's going to be okay?"

"It might be too early to know," Jillian said. "The doctor I spoke with said Gloria was in a coma. He didn't get to tell me much else, and I think he got in trouble for telling me as much as he did. He was really young."

Savannah nodded as she pulled the top from another cheese tray and set it beside the first. "When I was at the hospital not long ago, some of the doctors and nurses looked so young to me too." She smiled. "Did we ever look so young?"

"I happen to know we did," Jillian said. "And I have the yearbooks to prove it." Then the smile slipped from her face. "I'm starting to worry about Aunt Cornelia being involved with this movie. Things are getting entirely too dangerous."

"You know, as weirdly coincidental as it sounds, these could be accidents."

"Gloria didn't think so."

"You know she's one of my favorite actresses, but realistically, she is pretty old. Not every woman over eighty is as clearheaded as Bertie and Cornelia."

Jillian snorted. "I'm not sure you should hold up Aunt Cornelia as an example of rationality."

"Your aunt may have some unusual interests, but she's sharp as a tack, and you know it."

Jillian couldn't argue with that, so they worked together silently until the table was again covered with food, and the happy sound of munching surrounded them. Savannah pulled off her apron and handed it to Jillian. "I hate to abandon you, but the extras are supposed to gather in five minutes. I'm ready for my big debut."

"Actually I'll be glad you're out there where you can keep an eye on Aunt Cornelia."

Savannah squeezed Jillian's hand. "Try not to worry. I can't think of anyone who would want to hurt Cornelia, especially now that everyone is aware that it isn't Gloria out there."

If the person who had tried to drop a light on Cornelia was the same person who wrote on Gloria's chart, it was likely they'd finally gotten their real target. *But what if they're trying to stop the movie and not just the actress?* Jillian felt her stomach clench at the thought, but she smiled at her friend, knowing Savannah was trying to reassure her. As Savannah squeezed through the group in front of the tables and headed for the library doors, one of them swung open and a man leaned in. "Last call for extras for the street scene!"

At that, most of the people surrounding the table followed Savannah out of the building. The few left all looked familiar and a little sheepish. Jillian realized the library volunteers were taking advantage of the free snacks. She didn't mind. Since she'd reloaded, there should be enough for everyone.

Josi walked over to the table. "I don't know that I've ever had so many people in the library when no one was checking out books."

"I hope we're not scaring off your normal patrons."

"I imagine the closed streets are what's doing that. No one would want to walk too many blocks through this crowd and in this heat to get a book—not when they can wait a day and park close by. Besides, I like the sense of excitement today. It's contagious."

"It has been exciting." *Sometimes too exciting.* "Since I don't seem to have any actual film crew here and the tables are full, I think I'll duck out and watch the filming. Is that all right with you? I don't want you to feel like you need to man the tables. I'll be right back."

"Go . . . go." Josi flapped a hand at her. "I'd be out there with you if I could. You can tell me all about it when you get back."

Out on the street, Jillian slipped between two sweaty guys to reach a spot where she could see the actors on the other side. Annika and Kane strolled along the other sidewalk, her arm linked through his. They looked happy and relaxed. Jillian was amazed they could be so comfortable since they weren't dressed for the heat. At least Annika's cardigan was thin and her knit dress left her legs bare. Poor Kane's hoodie had to have him sweltering.

In a shadowy doorway alcove at the front of Tanner's Toys and Gifts, Cornelia stood glaring toward the two young people. The couple stopped so Annika could coo over the toys in the window. Cornelia stepped forward and delivered a line, though Jillian couldn't hear it from across the street. She was impressed with the menace her sweet aunt managed to convey with her scowl and unnaturally rigid posture.

Annika reacted to whatever Cornelia said by pulling away from Kane. She dashed up the street, pushing her way through a sudden crowd of extras walking along the sidewalk. The extras all wore dull expressions, and Jillian spotted Savannah right away, shambling along. Like the two young actors and Cornelia, all the extras wore warm clothes, which must have been particularly uncomfortable with them all pressed together so closely.

As Annika fought her way through the extras, cameramen shot her from different angles. The take ended with Christopher praising the actors and calling for the sprinting portion of the take to be repeated with a different camera angle. As Jillian watched, Annika ran away from Cornelia again and again, plowing into the crowd each time, pausing between takes so the makeup artist could dust sweaty faces with powder.

More than once, Jillian saw one of the extras slipping out of character with a smile. And once an extra tripped and tumbled to the sidewalk when Annika pushed her way through, but the extra was soon back on her feet with no sign of injury.

Jillian lost count of how many times they replayed the run through the crowd, but she was impressed with how much energy Annika kept up through all the physical exertion in the summer heat. Finally, the director was satisfied and called for a wrap. He thanked the extras for their work for the day and called the crew to be ready for a night shoot at Belle Haven.

Knowing that the end of the shooting would be a signal to eat again, Jillian headed back toward the library. It was even more difficult to push her way through the crowd of spectators now that they were moving. She felt like a fish heading upstream as she was jostled and pushed over and over in the short space of sidewalk.

Finally, she pulled open the library door, feeling as if she'd managed a major accomplishment. When she reached the snack tables, Josi asked her if she was all right. "I was watching you wade through all those people from in here. It looked crazy. What did that guy want?"

"What guy?" Jillian asked.

"The one in the hoodie," Josi answered. "He was right beside you part of the time, and I'm sure I saw him put something in your purse."

Jillian pulled her purse from her shoulder and jerked it open to check for her wallet. "I hope he wasn't a pickpocket. What did he look like?"

"I couldn't really see him in the crowd. Just a guy in a hoodie. Though I suppose it could have been a tall woman."

Jillian stopped and gawked at Josi. "A hoodie? In this heat?"

Josi shrugged. "That's what the person was wearing. He was kind of hunched over. Really I don't even know what made me think it was a guy. I didn't see the person's face at all."

"Maybe it was one of the extras," Jillian said as she continued to rummage through her purse. "They all had to wear those hot clothes." Finally she spotted something that looked out of place. It was a folded slip of lined paper. She pulled it out and unfolded it. Josi leaned close to watch and she gasped when the paper revealed a rough drawing of a crow with a red scribble across its chest. Next to that, in blocky letters, a message screamed out.

"The curse is real!"

10

Once the crew and extras poured in for a quick snack before heading back to Belle Haven, Jillian had no more time to stare at the note or discuss it with Josi, but she certainly thought about it as she kept the snack bowls full. *What was the note meant to do?* It certainly felt threatening, but she had to consider the possibility that it was meant to serve another purpose, like add legitimacy to the silly curse rumor.

Finally the last crew member fled the snack area to help with packing equipment for the move back to the mansion, and Jillian was able to clean up the tables. She thanked Josi for the use of the library.

"Promise me that you'll tell me what that note is all about," Josi whispered.

"As soon as I have it figured out," Jillian promised. "Until then, I would appreciate it if you'd keep it a secret."

Josi agreed, though Jillian could tell she was disappointed by the request. Jillian left, carrying a load of leftover food. She walked into the customer area of the bakery and found it bustling. Apparently watching the same scene shot over and over had built up an appetite in the spectators. Jillian knew Bertie would be glad for that.

She walked into the back of the room where Cornelia stood next to Lenora, commenting on the cake decorating the taller woman was doing. "Is that a bat? You should make it a raven. It better symbolizes my character, I think."

"What are you talking about?" Jillian asked as she paused at the table, setting the bags of food on the floor beside her. Her arms were grateful for the break.

Lenora grinned up at her, clearly unruffled by Cornelia's bossiness. "I decided to make a cake to bring over to Belle Haven this evening for your crew food table."

Jillian reached out to swipe a finger full of chocolate icing from the upper edge of a bowl on the table. "Craft services table."

Lenora waved that off with the pastry tube in her hand. "Whatever. I wanted to bring a cake to celebrate Cornelia becoming a movie star. Cornelia saw it and thought she'd give me a few tips."

Jillian looked at her aunt. "You do know that Lenora has been decorating cakes since before I was born, right?"

"But she hasn't been decorating *this* cake that long," Cornelia said. "And I thought it would be appropriate if the cake properly reflected my character."

"After seeing that dead crow, I'm surprised you want one on your cake," Jillian said. "That's kind of disgusting."

"I said she should put a raven on it, not a crow." Cornelia drew herself up as tall as her small frame allowed and gave Jillian a very Gloria-worthy glare. "I will not let some horrible prank ruin my feelings about my symbol."

"Your symbol? You remember this is Gloria's role." Then Jillian winced, as the image of the doctors and nurses huddled around Gloria came to mind. *I hope it's still Gloria's role.*

As if reading her mind, Cornelia said, "It may not be. My director said that I did such a fine job today that he could see me taking on the role completely."

"What are you talking about? You must have misunderstood."

"I don't think so. Christopher Dark told me he liked my performance so much he is considering allowing me to take over the role. He was quite clear."

Jillian felt a chill, even in the hot kitchen. Did the director know that Gloria wasn't going to be available to come back to the role, and if he did, was it because *he* made sure she couldn't come back? "What about Gloria?"

Cornelia's expression softened. "I don't want to take advantage of Gloria's accident, of course. I assume they'll let her out of the hospital tomorrow. Insurance never lets you stay very long these days, does it? Once she gets back, Christopher will forget all about me, I'm sure, but it's nice to imagine that I'm going to be a star."

"Actually, I don't know if she'll be back." Jillian told Cornelia and Lenora about what she'd witnessed at the hospital. "The hospital is claiming a mix-up, but I'm not sure I can swallow another coincidence. If someone is targeting this movie, I'm not sure you should get *more* involved with it."

Cornelia stiffened back up. "I believe the proper quote here should be, 'The show must go on.'"

"That's a big change," Jillian said. "Before you thought the movie was cursed, and the only answer was to shut it down."

"I believe I have the right to change my mind. Not about the curse. That's real. But about shutting down the movie. I've come to believe it's wrong to cater to these dark forces."

"Don't be silly," Lenora scolded her. "Curse or no curse—if someone is trying to shut down this movie and doesn't mind hurting people in the process, you need to walk away from that mess." She pointed the pastry bag at Jillian. "I know you're wanting to finish fixing up Belle Haven, but there won't be any reason to if you go getting Cornelia or yourself killed."

"So far, Gloria seems to be the target," Jillian said.

"Except for that big ol' light that nearly smashed into Cornelia," Lenora said. "I may be working back here and not gadding about, but I have ears. I know what's going on."

Before Jillian could respond to Lenora's last remark, her grandmother's voice cut through the air. "And what exactly *is* going on?"

"Someone tried to kill Gloria," Cornelia said. "Again."

Bertie folded her arms over her chest. "What are you talking about?"

Jillian caught her up on the experience at the hospital and then pulled the note out of her purse to show them. "Josi knows about the note, but she promised to keep it a secret, so I hope y'all will as well. I'm not sure if someone meant this for a threat, or if it's just meant to perpetuate the silly curse talk."

"It's not silly. Film curses are dangerous," Cornelia said and she began ticking off movies on her fingers. "*Poltergeist, Rosemary's Baby, The Omen,* even *The Wizard of Oz.* They were all cursed and all resulted in people badly injured or dying. It's a documented phenomenon."

Jillian stared at her aunt. "You carry a list of cursed movies around in your head?"

"I might." As Jillian continued to stare pointedly, Cornelia huffed. "Fine. I looked them up on the Internet at the library. I wanted to see if there was something we could do about it."

"And was there?"

"We could hire a shaman to lift the curse."

"You know one of those?" Jillian asked.

"Well, no, but I thought we might ask Pastor Keith."

Bertie pointed at her sister. "You will *not* ask the pastor of our church to break a film curse. The poor man is still confused from the time you wanted to bring the cat to church."

"Raymond always loved a good sermon," Cornelia protested.

"Don't start."

"I'm not afraid of you." Cornelia couldn't quite pull that line off believably. Everyone who knew Bertie was at least a little afraid of her.

Bertie turned to Jillian. "Curse or no curse, I don't like you and Cornelia in the middle of this."

"I'm not thrilled with it either," Jillian said, "but if we can sort out what's going on, maybe we can put a stop to it."

"That's exactly what I mean by putting yourself in the middle of it," Bertie said. "If that note was from whoever hurt Gloria, then that person clearly sees you poking around in this."

"So you think we should back out of the movie?"

Bertie and Cornelia both responded with stiffened affront, but it was Bertie who spoke. "No. The Chocolate Shoppe Bakery does not break a contract. But I do want you both to be very careful and sensible. Whatever is going on, leave it alone."

"That would be a first," Lenora said. Then she turned back to her cake decorating.

Jillian had had enough of the whole discussion. "If we're not breaking the contract, then I need to get back to Belle Haven and set up for dinner." Then she groaned. "This is the night that Wanda Jean and Maudie volunteered to bring something over." As always, the members of the Southern Sweetie Pies, Bertie's baking club, had been quick to volunteer to help out as soon as they heard about how much work the bakery and their friends were taking on. And getting their help had sounded good at the time. But Wanda Jean and Maudie were a force to be reckoned with in the Moss Hollow gossip circle.

"Then we won't say anything," Bertie said, catching Jillian's thought without further explanation. She knew Wanda Jean and Maudie as well as anyone. Bertie pointed at her sister. "Not one word."

"My lips are sealed," Cornelia said. "Now, if you'll excuse me, I'm going home. I am working on an idea that might help us find out what's really going on."

"No!" Bertie and Jillian half shouted in unison. They exchanged quick glances and Bertie spoke. "Cornelia, don't poke your nose into this. Just do the job you promised to do and stay out of trouble."

Cornelia put her hands on her hips. "My idea doesn't involve my nose at all. It won't put me in any danger. And since you're not the boss of me, Bertie Harper, I'll thank you not to tell me what to do." Then Cornelia turned sharply and stormed across the kitchen to the back door.

Bertie turned to Jillian. "You get home too, and keep your aunt out of trouble."

"I'll do my best." *And just pray it's enough.*

When Jillian got back to the house, she was happy to hear Cornelia had arrived ahead of her and had gone straight up to her room. *Perhaps Cornelia's idea consists of more smoking sage sticks or a nice conversation with Possum.* Jillian could only hope that was the case as she headed back to the kitchen to prep for the dinner hour.

In the breakfast nook, the craft services table was nearly empty. There was a single bowl of wrapped granola bars and water bottles resting in a bucket of freezer packs, probably far from frozen after a day of inattention.

Nearby, Christopher sat at one of the tables, going through a thick pile of papers with one of the water bottles close at hand. To Jillian's surprise, the director wasn't wearing his signature vest, though he still had on the black T-shirt and jeans.

He looked up as Jillian walked in and smiled. "Your aunt did a fantastic job today. She really helped us out." Then his smile faded. "From the call I got a little while ago, we may have to call on her quite a bit more."

"The hospital called you?"

He nodded. "It seems Gloria has taken a turn for the worse. They aren't even sure if she'll be able to rejoin the crew." He waved his hand over the papers. "I'm working out ways to finish the filming using Cornelia. I still think I can have Gloria do the voice-over later when she's had time to recover. Even if she has to be in the hospital for a month or so, it shouldn't kill us as long as we can get all the actual filming done."

"I certainly hope Gloria will be all right," Jillian said pointedly, noting how self-absorbed the director seemed to be.

"She's a tough old bird," he said, oblivious to Jillian's tone. "I'm sure she'll be fine, though this would have wrecked us if we hadn't found Cornelia."

Remembering the conversation she'd had with the hospital volunteer, Jillian changed the subject. "Are you familiar with Gloria's first movie, *Hexe*?"

He chuckled. "Of course. I'm a horror-movie director, and *Hexe* is a cult classic. Have you seen it?" When Jillian shook her head, he continued. "Gloria was fantastic in it. She had the same kind of innocence and fragility that Annika brings to the screen today."

"That reminds me of something interesting I heard today," Jillian said. "The actress who died on *Hexe* was named Annie Venture. That sounds so similar to Annika Venn. I thought it was an amazing coincidence."

Again the director laughed. "It's no coincidence at all. I picked Annika for the part as soon as I heard her name. I thought we might pull in some of the cult fans. They love that kind of thing. And Annika is doing a fantastic job, so it's all good."

"Other than these terrible accidents."

"Yeah, those are costing me a fortune."

"And hurting people."

The director folded his arms on top of the pile of papers and looked at Jillian mildly. "You think I don't care about people getting hurt? I do care. But I admit that I care the most about getting this movie done since that will allow all these many people to collect a paycheck for the work they've done. And I'm responsible for keeping it on track."

Jillian studied his face. "Do you wonder who might be responsible for getting it off track?"

He huffed and leaned back, snatching the water bottle off the table and unscrewing the cap. "Don't look for curses and conspiracies where they don't exist. You seem like a levelheaded person, Miss Green. The mishaps we've experienced are accidents. Every movie has them, some just have more. Luck of the draw."

"Maybe," Jillian said, "but I'm still not convinced someone isn't stacking the deck. After all, someone killed that crow in Gloria's room."

He took a deep swallow of the water before speaking. "I thought you said it flew into a window."

"That's what I thought, but I've checked most of the windows in the house, and I haven't found any broken glass. Plus, the door to Gloria's room was closed, as was the door from the bathroom to Annika's bedroom. Dying birds don't open and shut doors."

"Fine. Someone on the crew has a sick sense of humor. They probably found the bird dead and thought they'd use it to prank Gloria. She's certainly annoyed enough people. Gloria never met anyone she couldn't antagonize." He pointed his pen at Jillian. "There's another possibility as well. Those protesters were standing out beside the road yesterday. They easily might have seen a bird hit by a car and thought it would make a great warning for the big bad horror movie."

"Maybe," Jillian said slowly, remembering the woman at the hospital who may or may not have been one of the protesters. "Though you'd think if they'd done it, they would have left the bird in a more public spot."

He waved away the idea. "Who knows what goes on in the head of someone like that? Maybe they are among the many people who just don't like Gloria Baxter."

"Including you?"

"Of course. I'm only human, and the woman has been a pain since I agreed to put her in *Deadly Gothic*."

"Hiring Gloria wasn't your idea?"

He snorted. "Hardly. One of our backers is a fan. Of course, once I agreed to it, it did open all those delicious connections to *Hexe*." He sighed and gestured to the papers in front of him. "If you don't mind, I need to finish up here before the crew gets back from packing up. I was hoping to grab a few quiet minutes to work."

"I'll leave you to it."

"Thanks." He put down the water bottle and straightened his papers. Then he looked at Jillian and made shooing motions with his hands. Jillian walked back into the kitchen area and began prepping for dinner. She wanted to be ready when the food arrived.

While she worked, she kept an eye on the director at the table, her conversation with him turning over in her mind. He certainly didn't seem very concerned about Gloria, but Jillian couldn't see any real reason for him to have attacked the actress. Gloria was costing him money, but not having an actress for the role was sure to cost him even more. Of course, with Cornelia, he *did* have an actress for the role.

She thought about the director's choice of hiring Annika because her name was similar to the actress's in *Hexe*. Now the film had another similarity, with Gloria being replaced by Cornelia. If he truly thought links between *Hexe* and *Deadly Gothic* would sell tickets, the turn of events had certainly played in his favor. But trying to kill Gloria just to reproduce an event of an earlier movie was crazy. *Surely Christopher Dark isn't crazy.*

"You look deep in thought." Jillian looked up to see Leo Shone on the other side of the kitchen counter grinning down at her. "You looked like you were trying to stare a hole through Christopher."

Jillian pulled open a drawer and began pulling out serving spoons to cover up her embarrassment at being caught. "Anything I can get you, Leo?"

"I was just wondering if Bertie might be along soon."

"Someone else is fixing the main dish for dinner tonight," Jillian said as she piled the serving spoons in a bowl so they'd be handy later. "But Bertie will be along with dessert. It's going to be a cake to celebrate Cornelia's first day, along with a selection of mini-pastries from the bakery."

"That bakery is a fine thing," Leo said. "Your grandmother is an amazing woman."

"I think so too." Jillian smiled up at Leo. "You know, I'm going to have to broaden my horror-movie education. I saw you in that movie last year about the U.S. Marshals and the one about the ranch, but I don't remember ever seeing you in any horror-movie trailers. It seems kind of far afield of your regular roles."

He nodded. "It is. This is my first horror movie, and the role is pretty small. As a fella gets older, he tends to be disinclined to turn down offers of work. Plus, I've never played a bad guy before. I want to prove I can glower with the best of them. And since it's something I've never done, I thought it might be fun to try something new."

"I can see how that would be," Jillian said as she began rolling silverware into napkins and poking them into the basket to go on the food table. "Did you hear about Gloria?"

"That she's still in the hospital? Yeah, I was surprised when she wasn't on set today. That little bump on the noggin didn't seem like much yesterday."

"She's taken a turn for the worse."

Concern clouded the man's rugged features. "I'm sorry to hear that. Not that Gloria's exactly easy to get on with, but I hate to hear that she's taken a turn."

Jillian nodded, not sure she should tell him exactly what happened. Instead she changed the subject as she rolled another bundle of silverware. "Did you just get back from the shoot or did you stop by your room?"

"I didn't actually go to the shoot today," Leo said. "I wasn't needed so I hung around here. This is a beautiful old place."

"We're proud of it." Then she thought of something. "Since you were here all day, did you catch sight of the protesters at all? I noticed they weren't here when I left this morning or when I came home. It seems odd that they'd just go away when they were so gung ho before."

"I didn't see them, but I wasn't paying attention to the driveway either."

"Of course." Jillian shifted the rolls of silverware in the basket to make room for the last few. "Did you see Aunt Cornelia upstairs just now?"

He shook his head. "It was quiet as a tomb when I came down."

Jillian wrinkled her nose. "I never liked that particular figure of speech." She poked the last of the rolled silverware into the basket. "I want to run upstairs and check on her. She had a challenging day. If you're planning to wait down here for Bertie anyway, will you tell anyone who arrives that I'll be right back?"

"I would be happy to help in whatever way I can."

"Thank you. I'll be sure to put in a good word with Bertie."

He sighed. "I can use that sure enough."

Jillian patted his arm in sympathy then slipped around the counter and headed out of the kitchen. She was sure Cornelia was just fine. But she'd feel better after she checked on her.

She didn't see anyone else on her way through the house. *The crew must still be packing up.* The old house was quiet, but far from creepy with the bright light pouring in from the expanse of windows. As Jillian started up the stairs, the light from the stained glass dome gave everything a golden hue.

The second floor was as empty as the first though not nearly as brightly lit, with most of the windows inside bedrooms and bathrooms. She paused outside Cornelia's door and rapped sharply on the door.

Her knock was answered by a single, bloodcurdling shriek from inside.

Jillian threw open the door and rushed into the room, nearly barreling right into her aunt, who stood in the middle of the room cradling Possum. "Aunt Cornelia, are you all right?"

Cornelia stared at her. "Of course. Are you? You seem overwrought."

"I heard a screech."

"Oh, that was him." Cornelia lifted Possum slightly. "I stepped on the poor darling's tail when I stood up to answer the door. I hadn't noticed him jump off the bed." She gave the cat a tiny, gentle shake. "He was supposed to be helping me connect with the haint."

Jillian looked at the annoyed expression on the cat's face. "Possum was supposed to help you talk to a ghost?"

"*Raymond* was supposed to help me," Cornelia said. Then she sighed and put the cat gently on the floor, and he dashed out the open doorway. Cornelia gestured toward the bed. "Honestly, I cannot seem to make this work at all."

Jillian looked at the bed where piles of tear-out cards from magazines littered the floral spread. "Maybe you could walk me through how you were using tear-out cards from magazines to contact the Belle Haven ghost."

"It's an idea I got when Bertie and I were at the Clip & Curl. I was chatting with Lulabelle while she fluffed my curls a little."

"Lulabelle?"

"She works for Jasmine. Honestly Jillian, you should make more of an effort to be social and meet people. Lulabelle is a fascinating woman, and we have very similar interests."

"Her dead husband is a cat too?"

Aunt Cornelia gave her a withering look. "I would appreciate it if you didn't mock your Uncle Raymond." She pointed to Possum, who had returned and was presently rubbing his big head against Jillian's ankles. "You don't want to hurt his feelings. He has always been very fond of you."

"Of course," Jillian said. "Sorry, Possum. Now, exactly how does your chat with Lulabelle result in this pile of magazine cards?"

"Lulabelle is very open to unusual phenomena. She was telling me about this woman who advises her." Cornelia settled back down on the bed, her face alight with enthusiasm. "The woman apparently lays out tear-out cards and gets messages from the spirit realm from them. But I've laid these things out every way I can, and they don't seem to be telling me anything." She poked at one pile of cards, spreading them out to show a card from a true-crime magazine with a cover featuring a brooding teenager, another from a family magazine with lots of children and balloons, and a third from a men's health magazine that featured an issue with a handsome actor, someone with a far bigger name than anyone in *Deadly Gothic*. "I thought maybe the haint is trying to warn me about a healthy criminal who is from a big family, but I'm just not sure. It might mean that the crime will be solved by a cop with a big family and a health issue. These tear-out cards are very difficult to interpret."

Jillian stared at the pile. *Tear-out cards?* Then suddenly she realized what her aunt was talking about. "Aunt Cornelia, I think maybe you misheard . . ." Jillian stopped, not at all sure she wanted to explain to Cornelia about tarot cards. If Bertie thought she was encouraging her aunt, she'd never hear the end of it.

"I know you don't put much store in my sensitivity to the spirit realm," Cornelia said, "but you have to admit, we need all the help we can get. From what you told me about your visit to the hospital, I may be taking over Gloria's role for much longer than expected. And if I'm going to take over this role, I would like to know I'll be safe doing it."

Jillian thought it better not to mention that Christopher was planning exactly that. "I'm not sure how comfortable I am with you taking over the role considering someone may have tried to kill the last person who had it."

Cornelia folded her arms. "Women in our family don't run from a little danger."

"Fine. But please promise not to take any risks and don't go anywhere alone with any of the crew."

"I'm not foolish, young lady," Aunt Cornelia snapped. "Now, was there something you wanted?"

"I wanted to check on you. You had a hard day."

"Pshaw, standing around in funny clothes isn't a hard day. I'm fine." Cornelia looked pointedly at the clock on her bedside table. "But you probably ought to head downstairs if you're going to feed the crew."

"No one was there when I came up," Jillian said, "except you and Leo and Christopher. But you're right. I'm expecting Maudie and Wanda Jean. If I'm not down there when they get here, they'll talk poor Leo to death."

"And Bertie wouldn't like that at all," Cornelia said with a mischievous grin.

"Don't let her hear you say that." Giving in to a mischievous urge, Jillian reached out and tapped the true-crime card among the piles of cards on the bed. "You know, I think Gooder comes from a big family and he sure sulks like a teenager."

"I hadn't thought of that." She smiled brightly. "He could be the one to figure this out."

I hope he does it soon, Jillian thought. She headed out of the room while Cornelia turned back to the cards.

When she reached the ground floor, she could hear voices coming from the back of the house, so she picked up her pace. In the kitchen, Leo stood trapped against one of the counters as Maudie Honeycutt and Wanda Jean Maplewood grinned up at him and peppered him with questions.

"Do you know George Clooney?" Maudie asked. "I've always liked him."

"Now Maudie," Wanda Jean scolded, "just because they're both actors doesn't mean Leo knows him. I don't think George has ever done Westerns."

"I've done more than Westerns," Leo stammered.

"So you do know George!" Maudie asked, her shining eyes making her look even more like a white-haired pixie than usual.

"Good evening, ladies," Jillian said, pulling their attention away from Leo long enough for him to wriggle out from in front of them. "Have you brought us something delicious?"

"Of course. I whipped up mini-meat loaves from the recipe that won first prize in the Food for Less recipe contest last year," Maudie said, watching sadly as Leo ducked behind Jillian. "I popped the meat loaves in the oven to keep them warm. Wanda Jean just needs to make the gravy. She makes excellent gravy. I thought I'd chat with Leo while she fixed it."

Wanda Jean put her hands on her ample hips. "Now Maudie, you leave that cowboy alone. What would your husband think?"

Maudie gave a sniff. "He'd think he was glad I wasn't home interrupting his television sports. I was just asking Leo a few questions. There's nothing improper about *that*."

"Of course not," Jillian said, "but maybe you could help me with the dinner rolls. I bought some brown-and-serve rolls at the grocery."

Maudie gasped in horror. "You're not going to serve store-bought rolls? Bertie would burst a blood vessel. Here, let me get some biscuits going." She flapped a hand at Jillian. "I know where everything is, so don't worry about it."

In a flash, the two women were bustling around the kitchen as if they were in their own homes. Jillian saw Leo had retreated into the breakfast nook until he was close to the French doors leading onto the back porch. She walked over and spoke softly. "Sorry about leaving you to face that."

"Not a problem," he said. "I've faced bandits and rattlesnakes in the movies, so I think I can survive a couple of inquisitive ladies."

"When I walked up you looked a bit like you might be missing the rattlesnakes."

Leo chuckled. "Maybe a little."

As they spoke, Jillian heard voices outside the kitchen and soon a small group of crew members came in, looked pointedly at the food table before grabbing bottles of water and settling at the tables. Though they chatted with one another, they kept turning longing looks toward the kitchen. Jillian didn't blame them. The rich smell of gravy and meat loaf was making her stomach growl.

"Dinner should be ready right on time," she said, walking toward the seated crew.

It was a reassurance she made several times as more crew came into the house sporadically, some pointedly moaning and rubbing their stomachs. Annika walked in with Kane, who stopped at the counter and said, "That food smells fantastic."

Maudie and Wanda Jean, who had come into the room, beamed at him. "We hope you enjoy it."

"I'm gaining weight just smelling it," Annika said.

Maudie's glance took in the slender actress. "I think you can handle a few pounds."

"Now Maudie, that's not our business," Wanda Jean scolded, which nearly made Jillian snort. As best she could remember, that was the first time she'd heard either of the two women claim anything was *not* their business.

"I thought it was sweet," Annika said supportively. "Are you ladies relatives of Jillian too?"

"Oh no, not us," Wanda Jean said with a laugh. "We're all in the same baking club, which is why you're going to think you've died and gone to heaven the minute you taste Maudie's biscuits. In the Southern Sweetie Pies, she's a star."

Jillian knew the Sweetie Pies was filled with star bakers, and thankfully, they seemed eager to take turns helping out. As the crew continued to make eager comments, Maudie and Wanda Jean finished fixing the food, and Jillian set to work putting it on the table, sometimes finding a hand dipping in to grab a serving before she even let go of a dish. She had to admit, she hoped there would be some of the meat loaf, garlic mashed potatoes, and herbed biscuits left when they were done so she could grab a plateful.

When Maudie and Wanda Jean had first proposed the menu, Jillian worried a little that it might be too heavy for summer dining, but the hungry film crew certainly showed no sign of it. As she looked over the group, she noticed a conspicuous absence. "Has anyone seen Bibi today?"

Kane had just shoved a bite of mashed potatoes in his mouth, but he managed to speak around it. "I haven't."

"Neither have I," Annika said. "Not since breakfast. I'm surprised she was allowed to leave the hospital last night, considering her boss is *Gloria*."

"Oh?" Christopher said with amusement in his voice. He had cleared his papers off the table and joined in the eating as enthusiastically as everyone else. "Wouldn't you all wait anxiously in the hospital waiting room if I were there?"

"Dream on," Kane said, again speaking around his food.

I didn't see Bibi at the hospital, so where was she? Jillian didn't want to mention her own visit to check up on Gloria, but now Bibi's absence at the hospital seemed glaring. Of course, after Christopher had treated her like his assistant yesterday evening, she could sort of understand why Bibi would choose to avoid the house. Without Gloria there, Bibi might be enjoying the time off. She might simply not want to be roped into work for the director that she hadn't signed on for.

Before Jillian could give it any more thought, her grandmother and Lenora arrived with the beautifully decorated cake. "Run out to the van and fetch in the tray of mini-pastries," Bertie told Jillian.

By the time Jillian returned with the tray, Lenora was just leaving. She gave Jillian a quick sideways hug as she passed and whispered, "Stay safe."

Smiling slightly, Jillian walked into the kitchen and saw Cornelia had followed the noise downstairs and started in on dinner herself. Jillian was touched to see the crew include Cornelia in their group, chatting with her about the shoot and complimenting her first efforts at playing Mother Penn.

"It's not my first acting experience," Cornelia assured them. "I used to do summer theater back when my Raymond was alive. He and I once played Gatsby and Daisy."

Jillian heard her grandmother snort behind her as Bertie was laying the trays of tiny pastries on the table. She had to admit she had trouble picturing her rather plain, shy uncle as Jay Gatsby. It must have been quite a production.

"If you're done with us," Maudie called out as she walked out of the kitchen with Wanda Jean trailing behind her, "we're going to take off. It's bingo night at the volunteer fire department's auxiliary, and we hate to miss that."

"Maudie is a bingo wonder," Wanda Jean chimed in.

"I think we can handle the cleanup without any trouble," Jillian said. "Thank you both so much."

"We were happy to help," Maudie said, then dropped her voice and whispered. "Plus it was fun to see that cowboy making eyes at Bertie."

"He sure isn't subtle," Wanda Jean piped in.

"Not much," Jillian agreed. She found herself relaxing after the two older women left, not that she expected anything scandalous to happen over cake and coffee, but she really was glad not to add gossip to the mix of craziness from the past few days.

The sound of cheerful voices around her stopped all at once, pulling Jillian's attention back to the moment. She saw every eye turned to the doorway leading out of the kitchen. Jillian turned to find Deputy Goodman Jones standing in the doorway, looking around with a disapproving scowl. "Is there something I can do for you, Deputy Jones?"

"I'm looking for Bibi Bleu," the deputy said.

"Isn't that an interesting coincidence," Jillian said. "We were talking about her only minutes ago."

"And what were y'all saying about her?"

The deputy's tone made Jillian uneasy, and the uneasiness quickly turned to annoyance. "That no one has seen her since breakfast."

He looked over the room. "Is that right? None of you have seen Ms. Bleu since this morning?" He looked pointedly at Annika. "Don't you share a bathroom with her?"

"I share a bathroom with *Gloria*," Annika said, "but I believe Gloria insisted her assistant use the bathroom down the hall. The walls here are pretty thick, but Gloria knows how to project when she's giving orders." She deepened her voice to Gloria's gravelly tone. "'It is enough that I must share my bath with an actress of no consequence. I shan't share it with the help as well.'"

Jillian was shocked and felt a new surge of sympathy for Bibi. Gloria certainly couldn't be an easy boss, with her insulting sense of superiority. "I wish I'd known that bathroom was in use," she said. "I haven't even changed the towels in there."

The deputy's scowl increased as the conversation slipped away from him. "You can fiddle with your towels later. For now, I'd like someone to show me which room she was staying in."

"Those are private rooms," Christopher Dark spoke up. "Do you have a warrant to poke around in private rooms?"

Gooder's attention snapped to the director. "Do I need one? Because if I do, I'm not going to bother a judge to search just the one bedroom. I'll make sure it covers all of them."

The director smirked. "You couldn't possibly get a judge to sign a warrant for no reason."

"Oh, I think my uncle, Judge Haskell Jones, will sign quickly enough when he hears that Bibi Bleu is the one trying to kill her boss."

"What a ridiculous thing to say," Bertie snapped. "Gloria has been the victim of a series of terrible accidents."

"Brought about by the curse," Cornelia chimed in helpfully. The look from her sister suggested Bertie didn't find the addition helpful.

"Do you have reason," Bertie said, speaking louder as she took back the conversation, "to believe these were anything but accidents?"

Gooder nodded. "I found a note scrawled on the little notepad next to Gloria's bed at the hospital. It's pretty shaky, but I could read it well enough."

"And are you going to share what it said with the rest of the class?" Bertie asked.

Gooder reached into his back pocket and pulled out a folded piece of paper. "I had the note photocopied." He unfolded it and held it up. "Hopefully this will help you rethink the need for a warrant." The spidery handwriting was hard to read so Jillian stepped closer. From the sound of scraping chairs, she wasn't the only one with that idea. Everyone wanted a look.

As Jillian looked over the note, she wondered if Gooder was overstating its clarity. The paper was a mess of scratched out words and shaky handwriting. But the words she could read were chilling: "Bibi . . . wants . . . kill me . . . tell . . ."

The short note launched a buzz of conversation among everyone on the crew.

"That note could mean all kinds of things," Jillian insisted. "In fact, it may be addressed to Bibi, and Gloria was trying to tell her what she told me, that someone was trying to kill her."

The room fell silent and Jillian realized she had let the cat out of the bag in a big way. "Gloria told you someone was trying to kill her?" Annika said.

"Did she say it wasn't Bibi?" Leo asked, pointing toward the paper. "Because it certainly looks to me as if she's naming Bibi."

"It doesn't matter who she seems to be naming," Christopher snapped. "Gloria was forgetting her lines and wandering off set. The whole reason she was injured in the first place is because she got lost in your backyard. She isn't exactly clear-headed."

"Actually," Gooder drawled, "at the moment she's not clear-headed at all. She's in a coma, and they don't know if she'll make it. Now, may I please take a look at her room?"

Jillian sighed. "I can take you up to the room, but you should be careful about jumping to conclusions."

"Thanks, I appreciate your tips on how to do my job. Soon as we're done, maybe I can give you some baking pointers."

"That would be interesting," Bertie said and Jillian turned an annoyed glance her grandmother's way. *Really? Now you chime in?*

As they headed out of the kitchen, Jillian realized she had a parade following, so she turned around and held up her hands. "Y'all should go and enjoy the desserts from the bakery. I promise they're well worth lingering over."

"They'll wait," Christopher said. "If you think I'm going to stay down here while you rifle through rooms, you're mistaken. I do not give permission to search my room without a warrant, and I intend to watch and see that Barney Fife there doesn't accidentally wander in."

"Oh goodie," Gooder grumbled, "someone else who judges all Southerners by fictional people in Mayberry." He stalked away, and Jillian hurried to catch up. If Gooder wasn't going to try to keep the group from following, and Bertie's baking didn't tempt them, she didn't see how she would be very successful.

The second floor balcony hall was soon crowded with people, all squeezing in around Gloria's bedroom door as closely as possible. Jillian felt more than a little claustrophobic as Gooder waited for her to open the door and let him in.

The room was still perfectly neat, and the rollaway bed looked exactly as it had when Jillian saw it last. In fact, she saw no sign that Bibi had even spent the night in the room, though it was possible that she had simply cleaned up before she left. Gooder quickly scanned the room as he pulled on a pair of latex gloves. The bedside tabletops and the dresser top were empty of any personal items. Gooder walked directly to one of the bedside tables and began rooting through the narrow drawers. Jillian was glad to see he didn't dump them out or even disturb Gloria's belongings much.

After checking their contents, Gooder pulled the drawers completely out of the stand to look under and behind them. As he proceeded through the room, staying respectful and methodical, Jillian noticed that everything in the drawers and in the small closet belonged to Gloria; none of the clothes matched the style she'd seen on Bibi. *Where had Bibi kept her things?*

He finished his search of the bedroom and bathroom without finding anything other than a faint stain in the floor grout. "Crow blood," Jillian said. "I can't seem to get the grout white again."

Gooder just nodded at her explanation. "There's another bathroom, right? The one Bibi used. I assume you're all right with me looking that one over."

"Down the hall." Jillian led him out of the bedroom and wove through the gawkers. She noticed the crowd had thinned some during the search. Apparently, the lure of Bertie's desserts beat watching a closed door. "I haven't even been in this bathroom this week. I assumed no one was using it. We're bathroom-rich on this floor. When the family put in plumbing in the early 1900s, they went a little crazy with it. Though the way some of it works, I'm not sure it's been updated since then."

She opened the door and peeked in, hoping the bathroom wasn't too dirty, and wishing again that she'd known it was being used. It was actually the largest bathroom on the floor, as it was one that wasn't carved out of dressing room space. Jillian could only guess at what the room had originally been—maybe a small bedroom.

Now it was a large room tiled entirely in white, which gave it an industrial look. The room had a huge claw-foot tub that Jillian sometimes used when she wanted a long, hot soak. It was also the bathroom that gave her the most trouble with slow drains and stubborn drips. *Someday we'll get this one remodeled*, she promised herself. As Jillian's eyes moved over the room, she saw why they hadn't found any of Bibi's things in Gloria's bedroom. The woman's suitcase was crammed into the space between a built-in shelf unit and the porcelain sink.

Several nice blouses hung from one of the towel bars near the tub and Bibi had moved some of the towels on the shelves and put clothes there as well. "You know, I'm starting to not like Gloria very much," Jillian said. "I wish Bibi had said something to me. I'm sure I could have found her a more private place to keep her things. She shouldn't have to camp in the bathroom."

Gooder began carefully going through the stack of clothes, checking for anything slipped between items of clothing. "If her boss is as much of a tyrant as it seems, she might be used to it."

"I don't like to think of someone being treated this poorly, even if she is used to it."

Gooder shrugged. "She had a job and was staying in a nice old house. There are folks living in much worse conditions."

"I know." Jillian walked over to peek into the tub. The tub was so old that the porcelain was pitted in a few places, though not deeply enough to show the cast iron underneath. Despite that, the tub was immaculately clean, as was the sink. Clearly Bibi was as methodical as her boss, or else she was the one responsible for the cleanliness in Gloria's room, and was Gloria's maid as well as her assistant.

Jillian idly opened the medicine cabinet over the sink. The inside of the old cabinet was very clean, though the hinges were flecked with rust. A neat row of personal items lined up on one shelf: toothbrush, travel-size tube of toothpaste, dental floss, and a tiny bottle of mouthwash. On the next shelf up lay a small bottle of medicine and a syringe. For a moment, Jillian wondered if Bibi might be diabetic. "Doesn't insulin have to be stored in the fridge?"

"Yeah," Gooder said, turning to look in her direction. "My brother's wife is diabetic and that's where she keeps hers."

"Then why would Bibi have it in the medicine chest?"

Gooder walked over and carefully took down the tiny bottle in his gloved hand. "I don't think this is insulin." The tiny bottle had no label and Gooder frowned at it. "I need to take this with me. It's entirely possible we found what she used to try to kill Gloria Baxter."

He took a small bag from his shirt pocket and slipped the vial and syringe into it. He sealed it and wrote something on the label. Then he returned to his search of the room. It didn't take long. Bibi had few belongings. Finally Gooder lifted Bibi's suitcase up onto the sink and unzipped it. Because she'd laid her clothes on the bathroom shelves and tucked her spare shoes underneath the bottom shelf, the suitcase was mostly empty, containing only a few rumpled clothes and a couple paperback books, both romance novels.

"Looks like she may have been using the suitcase as her laundry hamper," Jillian said, gesturing toward the clothes.

Gooder lifted each item between two fingers to check it out. He stopped at a bloodstained blouse and looked at Jillian. "That's the one she was wearing the day Gloria hit her head," Jillian said. "I remember it. That's probably Gloria's blood."

"I'll take it with me."

"Do you need something to put it in?" Jillian asked. "I have a paper bag from the bakery."

"I don't need any cross-contamination."

"It's not a used bag. I brought a few home to try a paper-bag craft that I saw online . . ."

"You do arts and crafts?" Gooder grinned at that. "Well, isn't that adorable."

She narrowed her eyes at him. "It was for a display at the bakery. At any rate, it didn't come out looking like the one online, so I didn't do anything with the rest of the bags. Do you want one of them or not?"

"That would be a help, thanks." He looked at her. "Speaking of your room, how would you feel about my searching your room—well, all the family rooms, actually?"

"I feel like Bertie would immediately call your grandma and tell her you're out here looking through a lady's private things," Jillian said, folding her arms over her chest.

Gooder winced. "That's playing dirty. You know my

grandmother. She's got the pointiest fingers I've ever seen, and she's always poking me for one thing or other."

Jillian had seen Gooder's grandmother a time or two at church. The woman looked frail at first glance, but she had an iron will that made Bertie seem like a pushover in comparison. "You have my sympathy, but I doubt you'll have Bertie's."

"I'm confident that Bertie didn't kill anyone," Gooder said, "and I don't really suspect you."

"I'm touched."

He shrugged. "But, you were a suspect in a murder before, so if I have to get a warrant for a search, I can't leave you out."

"Fine, but you can leave Bertie and Cornelia alone."

"I'll have to include Cornelia." When Jillian opened her mouth to object he held up his hands. "She is part of the crew, and everyone knows she's as nutty as my Aunt Hazel's pecan pie. Some ghost or other could have told her to off Gloria."

"If a ghost told Cornelia to kill someone, she'd tell it no," Jillian said. "And then she'd sic Possum on it for good measure. My aunt is no killer."

"She's still crew. I won't be able to leave her out." He held up the small bag with the medicine vial in it. "But I'll hold off on any more searches until I have this analyzed. Maybe we'll find Bibi by then, and this can all be resolved."

Jillian leaned against the sink and looked sadly around the room. "I don't know. Doesn't this all feel a little too easy? If you tried to kill someone, would you stow evidence in the medicine chest of a public room? She may have been treating this like her room, but it's still just a bathroom and freely accessible to anyone."

Gooder openly smirked. "You think she's been framed? I think you just like conspiracy theories. You know, it's been my experience that criminals aren't all that bright or logical."

"But look at this room. Bibi is clearly a careful, methodical person. I know she has to deal with a myriad of details in her job, but when it comes to committing murder, she doesn't even try to hide the evidence?"

Gooder leaned closer, clearly trying to use his height advantage to intimidate her. "Why do you always have to complicate things?"

Jillian raised her chin and gave him her best version of the Bertie glare. "Because I'm less interested in simple than I am in true."

Gooder stood silently for a moment, clearly simmering. Then he took a step back. "You said something about getting me a paper bag."

"Sure, wait right here."

She stepped out into the hall and saw that even more of the crew had wandered off. Annika and Kane stood near the door that led to the library balcony. Intent on their conversation, they barely looked in Jillian's direction when she came out of the bathroom. Leo stood alone near the doorway to the narrow third floor stairs as if pausing on his way up to his room. At one time, the third floor had held only servants' rooms and storage, so the main stairs didn't continue to the next floor. Leo watched Jillian closely but didn't speak.

The only other person in the hall was Christopher Dark, and he stepped directly into Jillian's path. "I hope that deputy will be leaving soon. I must say I'm unhappy with you giving him access to one of our rooms."

"Gloria is in the hospital," Jillian reminded him, "and someone may be trying to kill her. If giving Deputy Jones access to Gloria's room helps to keep her alive, then I'm perfectly comfortable doing it."

"As long as your comfort level doesn't extend to any of the other crew rooms."

"Do you have something to hide, Mr. Dark?" Gooder asked as he stepped out of the bathroom, carefully holding Bibi's bloody shirt. The sight of it brought a gasp from Annika.

Jillian was happy to see at least someone was reacting to the horror of the situation. "It's the shirt Bibi was wearing when Gloria hit her head."

"Oh, right, I remember," Annika said quietly.

Gooder cleared his throat and gave Jillian a quick frown before returning his intense gaze to the director. "I asked you a question."

"One I do not intend to answer," the director said. "There is nothing wrong with valuing my privacy. The laws about search warrants are in place for a reason, and I see no reason to ignore them."

"Not even if it helps save a woman's life?"

The director waved his hand. "I've already given my opinion. Gloria Baxter is old and confused. And now she's the victim of hospital incompetence, which I suppose should be expected around here."

Jillian saw Gooder's face darken so she quickly interrupted. "I'll go get that bag."

She hurried to her room and grabbed a paper bag from the top of her dresser. Her hand had barely closed on the bag when she caught sight of the mirror over the dresser. On it, someone had written a message in bold, red letters: "Leave it alone!"

Without taking her eyes from the writing on the mirror, Jillian bellowed, "Gooder! Come here, please."

In the hall, she could hear conversation, and she had to call again before Gooder stuck his head through the doorway. "Am I taking orders from you now?"

"Look." Jillian pointed at the glass.

The deputy walked into the room and looked, leaning close. "I don't think this is blood."

Jillian shook her head. "No. It's lipstick. I recognize the color. I bought it for a costume party, but didn't end up using it because that shade looks horrible on me with my red hair. I kept thinking I should throw it away but good makeup is so expensive. Whoever wrote on the mirror must have gone through my things." As she spoke, Gooder took the paper bag from her and slipped the bloody blouse in it. Then he set the bag on Jillian's bed and turned his full attention to the note.

The deputy pulled out his cell phone to snap photos of the mirror. "When were you in your room last?"

"This morning. I had to get right to work on the craft services table when I got back here this afternoon and didn't have a chance to come upstairs."

"I don't suppose you locked your bedroom door."

"No," Jillian said dryly. "This is my home."

"And it's full of strangers," Gooder said.

"I know. I've been locking it while I'm in the room at night, but not during the day. I don't even have a key for the door, so if I locked it, I'd be locking myself out. Besides, I don't really have anything valuable in here. A little costume jewelry."

"It's interesting that someone directed a note at you," the deputy said. "Apparently your reputation for nosiness is spreading."

Jillian winced, suddenly remembering another note that she probably should have mentioned earlier. She pulled it from her pocket and told Gooder about finding it in her purse.

"And Josi said it was a man who stuck it in your purse?" Gooder said, staring down at the paper in his gloved hands.

Jillian nodded. "Though she only saw the back of the person, and she admitted it could have been a tall woman. She said he was wearing a hoodie."

Gooder seemed to consider that. "Have you seen any of the crew in hoodies?"

"In this weather?" Jillian shook her head. "I thought it might be one of the extras since they all had to wear long sleeves for the scene. *Deadly Gothic* is supposed to take place in October and culminate at Halloween."

Gooder held the paper up next to the message on the mirror. "Does that look like the same person wrote both?"

Jillian shrugged. "Maybe. They were both written in block letters."

"I can see some similarities. Look at how the crosspiece slants anytime the writer makes an *e* and the way the letter *a* slants just a little in both."

Jillian nodded as he pointed out the similarities. "Is that enough to prove it's the same writer?"

"Maybe. I'll get someone to compare them who knows a lot more about handwriting than I do." He frowned at Jillian. "This case involves a lot of notes. A note in blood, a note from Gloria, a note in your purse, and a note on the mirror. All by itself, that's weird."

"I wish it were the first time I'd ever gotten a scary note."

"You do seem to bring out the urge to threaten." Then he frowned at the two notes. "Though, really, not one of these was a threat."

"They're certainly creepy."

"Yes, but not specifically threatening. I wonder why that is." He narrowed his eyes as he pondered the notes. "Of course, technically, I couldn't charge anyone for any of them. With no threats, they are annoying at best. I might be able to argue a trespass charge, but since you don't lock your door, I don't know that it would go anywhere."

"So you think whoever wrote this is trying to avoid doing something illegal? Doesn't that tend to fly in the face of attempting to murder Gloria?"

"Not if the notes and Gloria's injuries aren't related." He rubbed at the slight beard stubble on his chin. "I just had another thought. We know of another group that would like to put an end to *Deadly Gothic*, but who seem a little worried about being arrested."

"The protesters."

He nodded. "I could imagine them looking for ways to throw a monkey wrench into the film without crossing enough lines to get them arrested. Collette Rawles sure seemed willing to cross the line yesterday."

"Collette Rawles?" Jillian echoed. "You know the leader's last name?"

"I am an officer of the law. After our encounter yesterday I looked into them. They have a website and everything, but they're mostly harmless, or have been in the past. This appears to be their first big protest, probably because Georgia isn't exactly Hollywood. Normally the group stays in Atlanta and writes angry letters and overly emotional Internet posts."

"How flattering that they decided to break with tradition to camp out at my house."

"Except I didn't see them when I drove in."

"I haven't seen them all day . . . maybe."

"Maybe?"

"Well, Collette Rawles is tall; I noticed that yesterday. I suppose she could have been the tall person in the hoodie that Josi assumed was a man. I did wonder why her group wasn't on Main Street protesting today. It seemed like a prime opportunity for it."

"All good points."

"Also, I might have seen her when I went to the hospital today to check on Gloria. I definitely saw a tall woman with that odd shade of red hair, but I wasn't able to get close enough to be sure."

"So, you could have been imagining things."

Jillian frowned at him. "I'm not that imaginative, you know. And if it turned out she was at the hospital, you'd be yelling at me for not telling you that."

"Unruffle your feathers. Telling me was the right thing for you to do. Not taking your dubious recognition skills at face value is the right thing for me to do too."

"Maybe you should go find the protesters instead of upsetting people here."

"Oh, good, more advice on how to do my job." He rubbed his forehead. "Why is it that anytime you're involved, I end up with a headache?"

Jillian chose not to rise to that bait. "How long do I need to leave this message on the mirror?"

"I've photographed it," he said. "I'll get a sample of the goo, and then you can clean it off if you want. At least I have plenty of things to keep the lab guys happy."

"Moss Hollow has lab guys?"

He rolled his eyes and snatched the bag of clothes from the foot of Jillian's bed. "Hardly. Our official coroner is your undertaker boyfriend. Of course we don't have lab guys. Well, unless you want to count Ed who thinks he knows everything because he watches a lot of Discovery Channel. Everything is sent off to the state lab guys."

Jillian considered setting him straight on Hunter being her boyfriend, since he wasn't, but she decided he'd only said it to get a rise out of her. Instead she walked out of her room and saw the group on the landing hadn't changed. "I think Deputy Jones is leaving now. You don't need to keep guarding your doors."

"I'm not guarding anything," Annika said. "I don't have anything particularly interesting or secret in my room. I just wanted to watch the fireworks if your deputy tried to get into Christopher's room and poke around in his secrets."

Jillian started to protest that Gooder wasn't *her* deputy, but Christopher spoke up. "I don't have secrets. It isn't a matter of having anything to hide. I'm simply concerned about protecting our rights."

"Sure you are," Leo drawled.

Christopher turned to him sharply. "And why are you here?"

"I'm here to watch over Miss Bertie's interests. She's a real lady and no one ought to poke around in her room without her permission."

"Such a neat excuse," Christopher said. "At any rate, I'll come downstairs as soon as the deputy does."

"Fine," Jillian said. "Y'all stand here and guard the place to your heart's content. I need to go downstairs and help with cleanup in the kitchen."

"I'll come with you," Annika said. She walked down the wide stairs at Jillian's side with Kane trailing behind. "What do you think? Do you think Bibi tried to off her boss?"

"I don't know," Jillian said.

"I can't really picture her putting the dead bird in the bathroom," the young actress added. "I'd have guessed her to be a lot more squeamish than that."

"Dead bird?" Kane said. "Do you mean the bird that flew in the window? Did Bibi chase it in or something? That's just mean."

"I haven't found any sign of a broken window, so I don't know how it got in."

"Unless someone carried it in," Annika said.

"You mean someone found an injured bird and didn't try to help it?" At the change in Kane's tone Jillian turned to look at the young actor. It was clear the thought of someone ignoring the suffering of an animal really upset him.

"The bird may have been dead when someone found it. We're only speculating. We don't know yet," Jillian said. "I admit I still haven't checked all the windows, but I'll get to them as soon as I can."

"You could ask Leo to check the third floor for you," Annika suggested, "since he has a room up there, and he's trying to score points with your grandmother."

"Maybe I'll do that."

When they reached the kitchen, Jillian was happy to see that while most of Cornelia's cake had been eaten, a few of Bertie's mini-pastries were left so the two young actors would be able to have dessert. Kane hurried to the table and picked up three mini-éclairs in a napkin and headed outside with them. Jillian hoped he could get them eaten before the heat melted chocolate all over him.

Annika didn't get anything from the dessert tray and simply walked to one of the tables where a group of young people already sat chatting.

Jillian looked over the few treats left and wondered if she should set some aside for Leo, or whether Bertie already had. Her grandmother was definitely softening toward him.

"Did Gooder find anything?" Bertie asked as Jillian began stacking the empty trays.

"A bottle of medicine and syringe in the bathroom Bibi was using," Jillian said. "She had her clothes and suitcase and everything in there. Apparently, the only thing she was allowed to do in Gloria's room was sleep, and possibly clean."

"Medicine?" Cornelia had walked over from the kitchen in time to catch Jillian's remark. "Insulin?"

"It wasn't marked, but it wasn't hidden either. It all felt very convenient. Plus someone left me a note on my mirror."

"Another note?" Bertie said.

"A brief one, in lipstick. 'Leave it alone.'"

"I was only asking."

"No, sorry, I meant the note. It said, 'Leave it alone.'"

Bertie huffed in something like a laugh. "Maybe Gooder left it."

That made Jillian smile. "He'd certainly agree with the sentiment. He pointed out that none of the notes have been overtly threatening. The first one was only ominous because someone wrote in the crow's blood, but the message was just the title of a movie."

"Unless someone German was actually accusing Gloria of being a witch," Cornelia suggested.

"Because that's likely," Bertie said.

Jillian jumped in before the sisters could really get going. "The note someone slipped in my purse wasn't exactly a threat either. I don't know what the point behind them could be."

"Well, the one tonight seems to be pointedly suggesting you stay out of this," Bertie said, "which might not be a bad idea."

Jillian reached over to the cake plate and used her finger to swipe a lick of frosting. "I don't see how. It's taking place right in our home."

"Jillian is right," Cornelia said. "All this negative energy is making it very difficult for me to concentrate on my role. Who knows what this movie could lead to for me?"

"One woman is in the hospital and another is missing," Jillian said.

The pointed remark flew right over Cornelia's head as she merely nodded. She looked over the table and then at Bertie. "Since the tea is done and you have Jillian back again, I believe I'd like to go upstairs and study my script for tonight's shoot. If you don't need me."

"We'll soldier on," Bertie said.

Again the sarcasm missed Cornelia completely and she merely nodded. "Excellent. I will see you all later." She paused at Jillian's side and whispered. "Don't worry, I will check the tear-out cards again, and see if I can get a message about these mysterious notes."

"Thank you," Jillian whispered back, and then watched as her aunt sailed out of the room.

"Do you think you can finish the cleanup on your own?" Bertie asked, looking over the mess. "I would love to go to my room and put my feet up."

Jillian winced inwardly at the amount of mess, but she didn't have the heart to ask Bertie to stay. "That's a good idea. It's been a full, strange day."

As soon as Bertie left, Jillian set into the cleanup with as much enthusiasm as she could muster. She not only had to clean up, but she also needed to set up a snack table for the night's shoot. Since she felt like whimpering when she thought of the work ahead of her, she focused instead on conquering each task.

Jillian had carried all but the last pan of treats to the kitchen when Christopher came in with Leo. The director clapped his hands loudly. "What's everyone doing sitting around? We have a night shoot to film."

One of the cameramen set down his glass of sweet tea. "It's all set up."

"Then let's go." Christopher looked around the room. "Where is Kane?"

"He went outside already," Annika said. "He's probably practicing with his ax, so he doesn't end up chopping off his own arm."

Jillian was surprised at Annika's mocking tone. She'd thought Kane and Annika were friends, but her remark sounded more like something Gloria would have said. She watched the group file outside, wondering if anything about them was genuine.

Christopher hung back and looked her way. "If you want to stay and finish the cleanup in here, you could just bring out a cooler of water bottles and a basket of the granola bars, if you have any. You don't have to man a big craft services table tonight."

"Are you sure?" Jillian said, surprised. "It's in the contract."

"I know, but we've put you through enough lately. And I appreciate your handling of the deputy." He turned and headed outside, leaving Jillian wondering about the sudden generosity. Then the door swung open again, and he poked his head back in. "Could you make sure your aunt makes it outside?"

"No need," Cornelia sang out as she swept into the kitchen with her Mother Penn costume back on. "I'm ready."

"So you are." This time Christopher actually smiled as he held the door open for Jillian's aunt. After the room fell quiet, Jillian finished cleaning up and even managed to sneak a piece of leftover meat loaf from the fridge to quiet her growling stomach. She pulled a bag of ice from the freezer and dropped it in the cooler before lugging it outside and setting it up on the paving-stone patio before running back in for a carton of water bottles. Setting up drinks and snacks took a few trips and Jillian was sweaty by the time she finished, despite the cooler temperatures in the backyard.

She walked back through the curving paths of the well-kept part of the garden. The humid air was almost too sweet with the mixed scent of peony, honeysuckle, and roses. When she reached the bustle of the film crew, she watched her aunt stalk toward

Annika and point a bony finger at the young woman. "You are nothing but a woman of loose morals."

"Cut!" Christopher bellowed. "Cornelia! That is *not* the line."

"I realize that," Cornelia said. "But there are some words a lady simply does not say."

"But Mother Penn isn't a lady," Christopher explained with tight patience. "She's an evil old witch."

"I'm still not saying that word," Cornelia insisted. "If you're going to record over my lines anyway, whatever difference does it make?"

"Your mouth movements have to line up with the actual words."

"It's dark. Who is going to see my mouth movements?"

Jillian watched the back and forth with some amusement, wondering if Christopher would begin missing Gloria soon.

"Fine. Can you at least mouth the word?" Christopher asked. "Without actually saying it?"

Cornelia thought about that. "I would still be saying it in my heart. Oh, I have an idea. Don't worry, I've got this."

After that, it was all Jillian could do not to laugh as her aunt inserted all sorts of odd words into the dialogue that sounded a little like the objectionable words and phrases. At one point, it proved to be too much for Annika who dissolved into giggles when Cornelia called her a "punch."

Leo stepped up beside Jillian, making her jump. "Your aunt is a joy."

"I'm not sure your director would agree," Jillian whispered back, and Leo chuckled.

Finally Christopher either got enough usable footage or he simply gave up, because he called for them to move on.

"Someone find Kane," Christopher shouted. "Tell him we're doing the first scene where Abby realizes she's losing him to Mother Penn's evil." He turned and pointed to Leo. "We'll need you for this one."

"I'm ready."

The bustle of movement picked up for a few minutes as cameras were shifted and the makeup artists rushed around powdering the sweat from faces. Through all the movement, Jillian noticed that Kane hadn't joined the group in the clearing. She wondered if he might have sneaked back into the kitchen for a snack since he'd not been in the previous scene.

She backed away from the group and headed back toward the house. She opened one of the French doors and yelped when Possum rushed by her, out into the darkness. The cat ran toward the tall shrubs at the back corner of the house and disappeared. "Great," Jillian muttered. She poked her head through the doorway, looking over the kitchen and breakfast area, but both rooms were empty.

I let the cat out for nothing. She headed toward the shrubs, determined to find the cat before he sniffed out Cornelia and managed to ruin a scene. Cornelia had harassed the director enough, Jillian didn't want to add a cat to the man's frustration.

"Possum," she called as she reached the shrubs. "Kitty, kitty, kitty."

Deeper in the shrubs, she heard Possum's low meow. "Come on, Possum," she said. "Don't make me crawl in there."

If the cat heard her, he clearly didn't care. Instead of coming out, he meowed again. Jillian crouched down and stuck her arm between the bushes, feeling for the brush of soft fur and hoping there was enough lingering scent of meat loaf on her hand to entice him.

Instead, her fingers touched fabric over something firm. *What is that?* She continued moving her hand over the fabric until the soft feel of cloth was replaced by cool skin. At that exact moment, Possum burst from the bush, slamming into Jillian's chest and knocking her backward onto her rump.

Jillian moved away from the bush. "Who's in there?" she demanded.

Whoever lay in the bushes didn't answer, and as she thought about the cool flesh under her fingers, she realized it was entirely possible the person never would.

In less than an hour, Belle Haven was a noisy rush of emergency vehicles and confused actors. Jillian watched, her hand pressed to her mouth as Kane Porter was pulled from the bush, his face so pale in the quickly strung emergency lighting that he looked like a ghost.

To Jillian's boundless relief, the young man was alive, though the expressions on the faces of the emergency crew made her wonder whether he would have the chance to stay that way.

"This is a nightmare," Christopher Dark moaned.

Jillian had to agree. "At least he's alive."

"That doesn't help *Deadly Gothic*," the director snapped. "I can't replace another actor."

Jillian turned to gape at him. "That's what you're worried about?" Suddenly all her tension and distress about the young actor and everything else that had happened in the last couple of days turned into a hot ball of anger. "I can't believe you can be that self-absorbed. Did you *see* him?"

Christopher took a step back in response to her anger and raised voice and his face flushed. With more space between them, Jillian spotted a familiar face coming her way. Deputy Laura Lee Zane strode across the lawn, her trademark ponytail swinging with each step.

Though the director was sputtering something at her, Jillian just stepped around him and walked toward Laura Lee. "It's so good to see you. I was expecting Gooder."

"He threw evidence at me as he walked back in from visiting here and left. From his grumbling, he was late for some family function. Since I was still in the office logging in *his* evidence, I caught this call," Laura Lee said, her expression turning sad as she looked around. "I love horror movies. I was excited to get crowd-control duty today, but I've still been meaning to come out and take a peek. I wish it wasn't under these circumstances. You found the victim?"

Jillian nodded. "Kane Porter. He's one of the leads in the movie. I was actually looking for Possum, and it was Possum who found Kane. He was crouched on top of the poor guy. Which considering Possum's girth, might not have been the healthiest thing for an injured man."

Laura Lee pulled a notebook out of her pocket, then shifted slightly to the left so she was standing under one of the outdoor lights. "You've gotten to know these people some, right? Anyone seem to have a beef with the victim?"

Jillian winced. "Can we go ahead and call him Kane? Somehow 'the victim' sounds so fatal."

"No problem. Anyone seem angry with Kane?"

Jillian shook her head. "No, Kane is sweet. Not exactly a rocket scientist, but really nice to everyone. The only person who didn't seem to like him much was Gloria Baxter, and she certainly didn't bash Kane on the head since she's still in the hospital herself, the last I heard."

Laura Lee nodded. "I skimmed Gooder's report. She had a head injury also, right? That's what put her in the hospital, and a med mix-up made everything much worse."

"If it was a mix-up and not an attempt on her life," Jillian said. "Did you know about the note she left next to her bed?"

"I saw a photocopy in the report. I know Gooder had it pegged as a clear accusation against Ms. Baxter's assistant, but I thought it was fairly ambiguous. Gooder talked to some of the nurses who tended Ms. Baxter, and they said she was paranoid in the extreme, accusing them of conspiring to kill her, so I'm not sure she's a reliable source."

"I didn't know what the nurses had said, but whether Gloria was paranoid or not, something fishy is certainly going on here. I don't believe Kane knocked himself unconscious in the bushes. I did see the note, and I'm not sure it pointed at Bibi; plus, I have trouble imagining Bibi Bleu attacking Kane. She is a good foot shorter than him, and slightly chubby. She definitely isn't someone you'd picture going up against a big, healthy guy like Kane."

"That could have worked in her favor. He wouldn't have been afraid of her."

"But why attack him?"

"You said Gloria didn't like him much. Maybe she had good reason, and it was a reason Bibi Bleu shared. If she wrote the note on your mirror—"

"You know about that too?"

"Of course. I logged in the evidence, remember?"

"Right, sorry, it's been a long day."

Laura Lee's smile turned a little sheepish. "To be honest, I've been following the case pretty closely." Jillian raised her eyebrows in surprise, and the deputy grinned. "What can I say? Any case you're involved in is almost certain to produce entertaining reports. As I was saying, if Bibi wrote the note, then we know she was around. She could be cleaning up loose ends before bolting."

"So she came back, left an attempted-murder weapon in plain sight in her medicine chest, wrote a note on my mirror, *and* bashed Kane in the head, all without anyone seeing her? That sounds more like *making* loose ends than cleaning them up."

"I didn't say it is a great theory. You said Gloria didn't like Kane. Any idea why?"

Jillian shrugged a shoulder. "She mostly made cutting remarks about his intelligence. I never heard anything more specific out of her until the day she was injured. Kane offered to carry her out of the garden, and she reacted really strongly to the idea of him touching her. I thought it was strange at the time, but she'd suffered a head wound. As someone who has had one of those, it doesn't exactly leave you with clear thinking for a while."

Laura Lee flipped her notebook closed and shoved the pencil into the spirals before slipping it into her pocket. "Who do you think attacked Kane?"

"I don't know."

"I didn't ask who you *knew*. What do your instincts tell you?"

"Keep in mind that my instincts haven't always been good." She stepped closer to her friend and glanced around to see to it they were far enough from any potential eavesdroppers. "I think Christopher Dark isn't above doing just about anything he feels is in his best interests. Gloria was slowing up filming and causing a lot of financial issues, but he seemed to be happier about it once Aunt Cornelia took over."

"Did he have a replacement for Kane?"

"No, which is a serious flaw in my theory. I think Christopher is capable of doing just about anything that he feels is in his own interest, but I can't see how Kane's injury is anything but catastrophic to the movie."

"You know, when I went to deputy school—"

"Deputy school?"

"Don't interrupt. One of the things I learned was to look at things like insurance for motive. Could the movie be insured? Maybe he's better off if it *can't* be finished."

"I don't know if there's such a thing as that kind of insurance, but *Deadly Gothic* is operating on such a shoestring, that I don't know how they could afford insurance like that if it did exist."

"Still, I think it's something I'm going to look into. If you have bad feelings about the guy, I'm putting him near the top of my suspect list. What do you think about Bibi, since she's Gooder's star suspect?"

"Gloria treated her horribly," Jillian said, "but I never saw Kane speak to her at all. Honestly, Bibi was easy to overlook since she mostly focused on scurrying around in the background while she fulfilled Gloria's demands or tried to smooth things over after Gloria got people stirred up."

"The person no one pays attention to is often the very best suspect."

"You know, I did notice one thing," Jillian said. "I ran into her washing her hands after I had carried the bloody crow outside, and before I discovered someone had been writing in the crow's blood on the bathroom floor. It's a reach, but I guess it could have been her who did the writing."

"A reach, but interesting." Laura Lee pulled the notebook back out and scrawled in it for a moment. "This is a lot of people. Anyone else stand out?"

"If we were talking about Gloria, there are plenty of people who didn't like her. She was horrible to the makeup team, vicious to Annika, and generally demanding of everyone. But Kane? He was sweet to everyone, and distraught about the crow. Honestly, if he had anything to do with the death of the crow, that guy deserves a major acting award. He just couldn't let that go, the idea that someone could leave an injured animal to die in pain."

Laura Lee perked up. "That could be the thing. If he actually found out who hurt the bird, someone might go after him for that."

"Sure, but this afternoon, he didn't know any more about it than I did. We talked about it after supper."

"So it was on his mind not long before the attack. Maybe he

had a thought about who hurt the bird, confronted the person, and got knocked on the head for his trouble."

"Confronting someone alone in the dark doesn't seem smart."

"No, but you said Kane wasn't the brightest bulb in the pack. And a big guy like him might figure he's invincible. Maybe the person he confronted was someone he liked or trusted, and he wanted to give the person the benefit of the doubt until he was sure."

"He seemed to have a close friendship with Annika," Jillian said hesitantly. "But this is speculating pretty wildly. I have been considering the possibility of the protesters being involved. You know about them, right?"

Laura Lee nodded. "Deputy Jones was quite colorful about them in his report."

"Well, I honestly thought I saw one of them at the hospital, Collette Rawles, and if she was skulking around the property after dark, I could imagine Kane confronting her, especially since he was worked up about the crow. I don't think he would have been afraid of a woman, even a tall one."

"I'll definitely see if I can track down their whereabouts, but can we go back to Annika for a moment? You said she was Kane's friend?"

"Well, I think he thought so but I heard her making unkind remarks about his intelligence when he wasn't around. Still, I can't picture Annika knocking him in the head."

"You said Annika and Gloria didn't get along, so she's a possibility to consider, but she's only about my age. Would she even have known what 'Hexe' meant?"

"She's the one who explained it to me."

Laura Lee pointed her pencil at Jillian. "Now that's interesting. I don't think that was in the report. I believe I'm going to ask a few nosy questions about all these possibilities."

Jillian nodded. "I know the hospital will keep the sheriff's department informed about Kane's condition, and Gloria's too. Could you let me know when you find out anything?"

The deputy nodded. "I will. And I'll say a prayer for them too."

"Thanks." Jillian felt bad that she hadn't actually thought to say a prayer for Kane's condition so she whispered one quietly as Laura Lee hurried off to question someone else. Then she began looking for her aunt. Though she could think of no reason why her aunt would be a target, she also saw no reason why Kane would be one either. The incidents simply wouldn't tie together in any logical way, and that meant Jillian would feel better when she saw Cornelia alive and well.

She tracked her aunt down near the French doors leading into the breakfast room. Cornelia and Bertie stood side by side, though they'd rarely looked less like twins with Cornelia still made up as Mother Penn. As she walked up, they were looking at Christopher Dark as he ran his fingers through his thinning hair, making it stand on end. "I can't make a decision until I hear back on Kane's condition. Clearly we won't be shooting anything tomorrow, so I'll give the crew the day off. You won't need to feed them."

"You, Annika, and Leo can join us for breakfast," Bertie said quietly. "Though we're early risers since we normally need to leave for the bakery around dawn. I'll leave muffins on the counter for anyone who sleeps in."

"That's kind of you," Christopher said, "though I doubt I'll get any sleep tonight. I don't know what's happening. This was going to be a simple, retro horror movie, and now I honestly don't see any way I'll be able to finish it."

"It's not your fault *Deadly Gothic* is cursed," Cornelia said gently. "At least, I don't think it's your fault. The tear-out cards aren't really very clear on that."

"Tear-out cards?" the director echoed, his face a mask of weary confusion.

"It's better if you don't ask," Bertie told him as she took her sister's arm. "Come on, Cornelia, we'll put on some decaf coffee for everyone." She half-dragged Cornelia through the French doors.

Jillian turned to Christopher. "Do you have any idea why someone would hurt Kane?"

The director shook his head. "He's a nice guy, and he's stayed out of all the trouble that young actors tend to fall into in our business. No drugs. No drinking. The animal rights stuff is about as wild as he gets."

"Maybe someone just wants to put an end to this movie."

"That's as crazy as the curse talk. *Deadly Gothic* is my fourth horror movie. They all had a decent run at the box office, mostly because they've always been timed to release at Halloween, but never anything earth-shattering." His voice trailed off and he just stood shaking his head slowly.

"You've put a lot into the movie already," Jillian said. "Are you going to be all right? Financially, I mean?"

"It wasn't my money," Christopher said. "And, honestly, most of my investors get into this kind of movie as a tax write-off. They don't expect to make money even if the film was completed."

"But earlier, you were worried about your investors pulling out," Jillian said. "Why would they pull out if they don't care about profits?"

"It's one thing to invest in a movie that you don't expect to make money, and another thing entirely to have your name tied to a cursed movie. Most of my investors really don't like that kind of press." He sighed and ran his hand through his hair again. "I'm going to have to bid you good night. I have a lot of thinking to do before morning."

"Of course," Jillian said quietly. She stood still and watched the director shuffle away. Though Christopher Dark couldn't be more than ten years older than Jillian, the events of the last few days seemed to have added another decade to him. He certainly didn't seem like a man successfully pulling off some nefarious plot, but *someone* was hurting people. More and more, Jillian felt like she had better find out who, before someone turned up dead.

Breakfast the next morning was subdued with everyone still feeling the shock of Kane's attack. All the empty tables in the breakfast nook and family room area underscored the strangeness. The smallest table that sat closest to the kitchen area easily held the few people still staying at Belle Haven. It was the only table that wasn't a rental, and they'd tucked it next to the only window in the room that looked out on the side yard instead of the backyard. The view wasn't one of Belle Haven's best as there were no garden beds on that side.

Of course, no one seated at the table was interested in flowers. The crew clutched coffee mugs as if they depended on them to live. Annika's eyes were puffy and red, while the rest of her face looked nearly as pale as the cream-colored T-shirt she wore. Neither of the men looked like they'd been crying, but Christopher replied to all remarks with little more than grunts. Leo's tanned skin had a gray cast. While Bertie filled Leo's coffee cup for the second time, he barely looked at her—something that hadn't happened since the moment he'd first met her.

Bertie and Cornelia had tried to lift the mood with amazingly light, fluffy pancakes, a luxury usually reserved for Sunday morning before church, but no one showed much appetite.

"You'll want to try some of this maple syrup," Cornelia said as she put the small jug on the table in front of Leo. "It comes straight from Stony Point, Maine. I get a bottle every year at Christmas from my late husband's cousin Annie."

Leo managed a faint smile at that. "I've never been to Maine."

"It's pretty," Cornelia said, "for someplace that isn't the South."

"I can't believe you're talking about syrup!" Annika snapped, pushing her virtually untouched plate away from her. "We don't even know if Kane is going to be all right."

"It's not the syrup's fault that Kane is in the hospital," Bertie said as she poured the final bit of batter on the griddle. "And refusing to eat won't make him feel better. If today is going to be tough, you'll all be best served to face it with a good breakfast in your stomachs."

"I don't know what today will be," Christopher said. "I tried calling the hospital this morning, but they won't give out information to anyone who isn't family."

Annika looked up, her gaze flicking from Cornelia to Jillian to Bertie. "You all seem to know everyone around here. Isn't there someone who can tell us how Kane is doing?"

Over the edge of her coffee cup, Jillian saw Cornelia and Bertie exchange looks. "Laura Lee would know," Cornelia said.

"Likely," Bertie agreed as she flipped another pancake. Her gaze flicked to the clock on the wall. "She won't be in the office this early though, not after working last night."

Cornelia walked back over to the counter and picked up a jar of jam. "We could call her at home."

"Did y'all notice what time it is?" Jillian asked. "I don't think Laura Lee would thank us for getting her out of bed."

"She isn't a late sleeper," Bertie insisted. "I see her running sometimes on the way in to the bakery."

"Can you call her?" Annika's voice was eager and spots of color had bloomed in her cheeks. Jillian couldn't bring herself to shoot down the young woman's hopes. Apparently Annika had cared more for Kane than Jillian had thought.

"It would help," Christopher said. "I can't even begin damage control until I know."

"That's right," Bertie agreed. "And then we can adjust plans for meals and such."

Jillian cast a last longing look at the hot coffee in her mug, then put it on the counter. "Of course." Her phone was in the pocket of the white slacks she was wearing since she planned to head into the bakery with Bertie. She had all the members of the Sweetie Pies in her contact list, so she quickly called her friend. Laura Lee answered the phone with such a cheerful greeting that it was obvious Jillian hadn't woken her.

"I have a lot of worried folks here," Jillian said, "and we can't get any news on Kane's condition since none of them are kin to him."

"So you were just hoping I might find that out for you."

"We were."

"Tell her there's a free chocolate éclair in it for her," Bertie called out.

"I heard that. I'll make a call and see what I can find out. Then I'll ring you right back. Tell Bertie I'll collect my éclair later today."

"Thanks. We really appreciate it," Jillian said.

When the call ended and she looked back at the group around her, she saw clear relief and gratitude on the faces of Annika and Christopher, but Leo just looked worried. He was older, so maybe more than the others, he knew just how bad the news might be when Laura Lee got back to them.

"Thank you, Jillian," Bertie said briskly as she put the last pancake on a platter and carried it to the table. "Now that we know someone will be getting back to us with news, I think you should all eat something." When Annika started to open her mouth, Bertie added, "Even if you feel like you can't. Hunger never made anyone deal with stress better."

With that pronouncement, she sat down and put two of the pancakes on her own plate. Everyone followed suit, and Jillian smiled at the power of her grandmother when she was giving orders. Even so, no one ate much, and conversation was practically nonexistent. It was a painful contrast to the boisterous meals they'd had ever since the film crew descended on them.

Bertie finally put her fork on her plate and dabbed at her lips with her napkin. "Jillian, you should stay here until you hear back from Laura Lee. I need to leave for the bakery."

"Are you sure?"

"I planned around you being here anyway," Bertie said. She turned to Christopher. "You said we should suspend food service, so we will until you decide otherwise, but if any of you get hungry, there are plenty of leftovers in the fridge. You'd be doing us a favor by eating them."

"Thank you," Christopher said. "You're very kind."

Bertie snorted. "Just realistic." She turned to her sister. "Are you planning to keep out of trouble today?"

Cornelia drew herself up stiffly in her chair. "I'm not a child in need of directions from you, but I plan to stay here today and do a little gardening." Then her expression brightened. "In fact, my garden club is having a meeting, and I wasn't planning to attend, but now I can."

Annika put down her fork with a sharp clink. "It's nice that Kane accommodated you so well."

"Listen here, Missy," Bertie snapped. "I know you're worried about your friend. We all are. Kane is a sweet boy. But you may not take it out on my sister, you hear?"

The two women locked eyes and, for an instance, Jillian thought Annika might argue with Bertie, but the young actress gave in first, dropping her eyes and mumbling something.

Bertie rose from her seat. "I'll see you later at the bakery, Jillian, and I imagine I'll see everyone else this evening." With that, she swept out of the room. Once again, Jillian was surprised at Leo's lack of response, not evening bidding Bertie good-bye.

"I hate to leave you with cleanup," Cornelia said as she laid her own napkin on the table, "but I would like to get started outside before the heat drives me back inside."

"No problem." Jillian stood and began piling Bertie and Cornelia's plates on her own. "You go on. There isn't that much cleanup."

Cornelia gave her a peck on the cheek and whispered in her ear. "Come let me know when you hear about Kane."

"I will."

Christopher stood then. "I would like to go to my room. Would you mind coming up when you hear back about Kane?"

"Of course."

"I could help you here," Annika offered with a shrug. "I don't have anything else to do really, and I'd just be hanging around the kitchen anyway to wait for the call."

"I'd appreciate the help." Jillian turned to Leo. "What do you have planned for the day?"

The older man jumped slightly, as if surprised to be spoken to. "Excuse me?"

"Do you have plans for the day?" Jillian asked.

Leo stood and stuck his hands in the pockets of his worn jeans. "I want to hear about Kane, but I can't stay inside. Maybe I'll go see if Cornelia would like my help."

"I'm sure she'd appreciate that."

He bobbed his head and headed out the French doors leading out onto the back porch. Jillian carried the plates and silverware to the sink while Annika trailed behind her with the coffee mugs.

"You and Kane must be close," Jillian said.

Annika froze. "What makes you say that?"

Jillian gently took the mugs from her. "You're clearly very upset."

"We all are."

Jillian stepped back toward the table to give the young actress a little space. She was confused by Annika's defensive responses. Finally she spoke, even more gently this time. "But you're the only one who has been crying."

Annika ignored the comment and walked to the table. She gathered the discarded napkins, then held the bundle in her hand and looked around helplessly. "I don't know what to do with these."

"You can leave them on the counter. I'll throw them in the wash." Jillian tried again. "You know, you might feel better if you talked about it."

"I doubt that," Annika said, then sighed, a long shuddery sigh. "If I tell you a secret, will you keep it to yourself?"

"If it's a secret that doesn't hurt anyone."

Annika looked at her in surprise. "Of course it is. I just . . . We didn't want anyone to know."

"To know what?" Jillian asked.

Annika paused, turning away from Jillian to scoop the maple syrup from the table. "Where does this go?"

"Fridge," Jillian said. "You didn't want anyone to know what, Annika?"

Annika held the small jug of syrup, the outside moist with condensation. "To know that Kane and I were involved. We haven't been seeing each other long, and we didn't want Christopher to turn it into a thing. That kills so many relationships, the way they turn into a *thing*, with publicity pictures and no privacy. We didn't want that."

"I understand," Jillian said. Then she remembered Annika's remark of the other night. "But you seemed to be making fun of him last night, when you talked about him practicing with the ax."

Annika waved that off. "Kane knows he's a klutz; he's not sensitive about it. And I was mostly trying to make sure everyone saw us as just coworkers." Suddenly her eyes filled with tears and her next words came out thick. "I wouldn't have said it if I'd known."

"I'm sure he would understand."

Annika offered a weak smile. "Thanks." She carried the jug of syrup into the kitchen. Jillian looked over the table to see if they'd missed anything. *It will need a good wiping.* Her eyes strayed to the side yard window and her attention was captured by what she saw. Leo stood at the corner of the porte cochere, gesticulating wildly at someone. *Surely Cornelia hasn't worked him up like that.* Jillian shifted position to see who was on the receiving end of Leo's wrath. She had to practically press her face to the window to catch a glimpse of the woman half-hidden in the shadow of the porte cochere, but she didn't need more than a glimpse to recognize the burgundy-colored hair. Collette Rawles was back on their property!

"**E**xcuse me a minute, Annika," Jillian said as she stormed through the kitchen and the laundry room to reach the side door that opened on the porte cochere. She flung the door open hard enough to make it bang, and both Collette and Leo startled.

"What are you doing back on our property?" Jillian demanded.

Collette folded her arms, resting them on the large camera she wore on a strap around her neck. "Trying to find out what's going on. I heard some of the crew talking at the breakfast buffet this morning." Her lips quirked into a smile. "Is the movie actually dead?"

"I can remove her if you want," Leo offered.

Collette pointed a perfectly manicured finger at him. "You touch me, and I'll have you arrested!"

"You might as well leave. I'm not going to talk to you about the movie," Jillian responded. "I'll give you a chance to get off the property before I call the sheriff's department. And I can assure you that it won't be Leo who ends up in cuffs."

Collette held up her hands. "Calm down. I haven't done anything. I don't even have a sign."

"I noticed you still have your camera, but you must have left your minions back at the hotel."

The other woman scowled. "Hardly. They scurried back to Atlanta after your pet deputy threatened to arrest us. Cowards and turncoats, every one of them."

"Leaving you free to skulk around," Jillian said. "I saw you at the hospital."

The other woman visibly paled. "I don't know what you're talking about."

Out of her peripheral vision, Jillian saw Leo take a step back. She hoped he was giving her room to confront the woman and not just trying to distance himself from Jillian's behavior. She pushed aside that concern and took another step closer to the protester. "It was the day someone tried to kill Gloria. You were at the hospital. I saw you. And I've already told the deputy that I saw you."

"It couldn't have been me," she said, her nervous shifting making it clear that she was lying. "I wasn't there."

"You were. What I want to know is why. Are you the person who altered Gloria's medical chart? Or maybe you just injected her and then altered her chart. And later you trespassed here, just like you're doing now, and left the medicine in my house."

"That's ridiculous."

Jillian pulled her phone out of her pocket. "Let's see if Deputy Jones thinks it's ridiculous."

The woman held up a hand. "Fine. I was there, but I didn't do anything to Gloria Baxter's meds. I just wanted a photo of her."

"A photo?" Jillian gawked at her. "You went to the hospital to take a photo of a woman lying in a hospital bed?"

"Of an *actress* in a hospital bed. Sure, she's a faded star these days, but the photo would still have been worth a few bucks."

"I don't understand."

"Paparazzi," Leo explained. "She takes pictures of actors minding their own business and sells them to tabloids. Am I right?"

Collette went back on the offensive, pointing a finger at Leo. "Hey, I have to pay for our organization's expenses somehow. If we tried to rely on the bake sales and basket raffles the rest of them come up with, we couldn't keep the lights on in our office."

"So you took a photo of Gloria?" Jillian said.

The taller woman shook her head, making her purplish curls bounce. "I intended to. I had the perfect shot. The old woman was scribbling on some notepaper and didn't even see me. It would have been perfect. But then I heard someone coming out of the bathroom, and I didn't want to be caught. Hospital security can be overzealous. I've heard of cameras being destroyed, and this one cost me a fortune."

"Did you see who was in the bathroom?" Leo asked.

"No. I jumped back as soon as I heard the sound of the door. I figured I'd just go downstairs and have a cup of coffee, then try again. I mean, how long could someone visit with a person like Gloria Baxter? I planned to just catch her alone later."

"Did you?" Jillian asked.

Collette shook her head. "When I came back, there was all that commotion and I saw *you*." She gestured toward Jillian. "I didn't want you calling Deputy Dawg and getting me thrown out, so I ducked into the chapel. I got caught by some preacher who wanted to give me comforting words." She rolled her eyes. "By the time I got out of there, you were gone and I couldn't get anywhere near Gloria's room. So I gave up and came back to Moss Hollow. I took a few photos on Main Street but the crowd was crazy, and I didn't get anything usable."

"Were you wearing a hoodie?" Jillian asked.

Collette laughed. "In this heat? Hardly."

"I believe the deputy still wants to talk to you," Jillian said. "And he'll want to hear what you just told me, in light of what happened to Gloria later."

The taller woman huffed. "I'm not going to jail. I didn't do anything."

"Surprisingly, I believe you, but he's still going to want to hear about what you saw."

"Which was nothing."

"You saw Gloria writing the note that was found on her nightstand. You saw that no one was standing over her making her write it," Jillian said.

Collette raised her eyebrows. "That note was something special?"

"Maybe the deputy will tell you about it." Jillian turned her attention to her phone, thinking she'd call Laura Lee instead of Gooder. It might be his case, but she had no desire to talk to him herself.

While Jillian's attention was diverted, Collette Rawles made a run for it, dashing off at a surprising speed. Jillian shoved the phone in her pocket and ran after her, but the combination of Collette's longer stride and clear evidence that she was in better shape let her leave Jillian far behind on the driveway. Jillian managed to see the taller woman jump into an SUV and drive off. As Collette turned the large vehicle around, Jillian caught sight of the vanity plate, HIH CR. *Well, that will be easy to remember.*

Puffing heavily, Jillian headed back to the house. For an instant, Jillian wondered if she should take up running for situations like this, but then she felt the sweat trickling under her light blouse and decided there were worse things than losing a footrace. She called Laura Lee.

"Hi, Mom," her friend said cheerfully, "I'm in the middle of a work discussion with a colleague. Can I call you back?"

"Tell Gooder that Collette Rawles was just here. She was at the hospital before Gloria's condition got bad and saw her writing the note. She also heard someone in Gloria's bathroom. It might have been the attacker."

"Is she there with you now?" Laura Lee asked, all the false cheer gone from her voice.

"No, I tried to detain her, but she runs a lot faster than I do."

"That explains the wheezing. Hold on, you better tell this to Deputy Jones directly." Jillian heard Laura Lee's voice change as she held the phone away from her face. "You need to take this. It's Jillian Green."

"Oh?" Gooder drawled. "What's she doing visiting your mother?"

Jillian didn't hear Laura Lee's response, but Gooder was chuckling when he spoke into the phone. "What fresh catastrophe do you have for me this morning, Miss Green?"

"You'd be sorry for your flippant tone if I actually had a fresh catastrophe. Leo Shone caught Collette Rawles skulking around the property." She repeated everything she'd told Laura Lee.

"Is she there?"

"No, she ran off rather than chat with you. But she's driving a dark SUV, and I got the plate number." She rattled it off. "She said she overheard the crew talking this morning, so that means she's staying at the Raindrop. If you want to catch her, you might want to head on out there."

"Still telling me how to do my job, I see. Thanks for this. To show what a good sport I am, I'll give the phone back to Laura Lee so you can pump her for information. I'm going to go catch a paparazzi."

"You know I'm going to catch all kinds of grief later," Laura Lee said as soon as Gooder handed her back the phone. She didn't sound particularly worried about it.

"Sorry," Jillian said. "I was trying to avoid talking to Gooder, though he's in an unusually good mood."

"We caught some good news. Gloria and Kane are both awake. The hospital flatly won't let us talk to them yet. They're both pretty weak, but it looks like we're not going to have any fatalities this time."

"That's fantastic!" By now Jillian had reached the porte cochere where Annika had come out to join Leo.

"You know it. Look, I have to run. Gooder wants me to drive out to the hospital to keep an eye on the patients. We don't want any repeats of Gloria's medical mishap."

"Good thinking. Thanks so much."

She ended the call and quickly repeated the good news to Annika and Leo. Annika burst into happy tears, and Leo put a fatherly arm around her.

"Can I see him?" Annika asked.

"Apparently they're not letting him have visitors. The medical staff won't let Gloria or Kane speak to the police about what happened until they're stronger."

"I'm going to drive out to the motel and let the rest of the crew know," Leo said. "I know they've been as scared as we have."

"That's nice of you," Jillian said, then watched as Leo strode away. She turned back to smile at Annika. "I don't know if you have a car here, but I can drive you to the hospital if you'd like."

"I would." She rubbed at her eyes with the heels of her hands. "But I think I'll wait until they're letting him have visitors. I'm not a relative, so if they aren't letting the police talk to him they're not going to let me visit. And I hate hospitals. Just sitting around in a waiting room would be awful."

"I understand. Well, I'd better get back to cleaning up the kitchen."

"I'll help." Annika took a deep shaky breath. "Wouldn't it be great if this was all over?"

"But it's not." Jillian turned to see Cornelia walking toward her with one of her floppy gardening hats perched on her head. "It's not over at all."

"What are you talking about?" Jillian asked her aunt.

"You'd better come and see for yourself."

Jillian and Annika trailed after Cornelia. She walked along the side of the house and pointed. A tall oak stood about halfway from the house to the road. Jillian remembered the tree well from when she was a little girl. She would climb up into its branches and read a book in the cool shade. "The oak tree spoke to you?" she guessed.

"Don't be ridiculous."

That's when Jillian noticed that the wild grapevines that had always grown on the fence there had apparently leaped the gap and now wove up the tree. She could see clumps of grapes hanging. "Grapes? Are they bad luck or something?"

"Good heavens, Jillian, not the grapes. The ravens!"

Jillian took a few steps closer to the tree. Sure enough, a number of black birds picked at the grapes dangling from the vines. "I'm pretty sure those are crows."

"They're ravens, and I already told you that they are a link to the spirit realm. I believe they're being drawn to the house by the coming misfortune."

"Or the grapes," Annika said.

Cornelia gave the young actress a slightly pitying look. "You're not Southern, so I'm sure you don't know about such things, but Jillian shouldn't be so scornful. I saw a raven outside the hospital window on the day my dear Raymond passed."

Jillian looked at the crows in the tree. "I do suppose this partially explains the crow that ended up in Gloria's room. It was probably here for the grapes. Though we still don't know how it got in the house."

"You're ignoring the most important clue of all," Cornelia said, waving her hands and raising her voice so much that the crows startled and took flight, squawking as they flapped into the air.

"I don't suppose I'll see it now that you scared the crows away."

"Ravens," Cornelia snapped. "Thirteen ravens. And if that doesn't mean something bad is coming, I don't know what does."

"Thank you for warning us," Annika said consolingly. "We'll be more careful."

Cornelia narrowed her eyes as she looked closely at Annika, unsure if she was being mocked. "You should be." She pointed her garden shears at Jillian. "Since you don't intend to pay attention to clear signs, I'm done trying to get through to you. I'll be in the living room with a glass of sweet tea if you need me." With that, she swept regally away.

Once she was out of hearing, Annika giggled. "Living with Cornelia must be fun."

"That's one word for it," Jillian said. "Actually both my aunt and my grandmother are the finest women I know, but they are stubborn and opinionated."

"All strong women are," Annika said. "So, are we heading back to the kitchen?"

Jillian nodded, but she looked at the house for a moment. "I think I'm going to take a walk around the house first. I really never did check every window for breakage, and I wonder if that might have been what Kane was doing last night."

"Sounds good. I'll come with," Annika said.

They walked slowly around the house, keeping enough distance so they could clearly see the windows on all three levels. All the windows on the front of the house looked fine, so they crossed to the side where Kane had ended up in the bushes. Jillian stared up at the windows for a long time.

"None of them are broken," Annika said.

Jillian pointed upward. "Does that second window on the third floor look funny to you?"

"It doesn't look broken."

"No," Jillian said slowly. "Not broken. Just funny."

Annika stared at it with her for a moment, then said, "It looks like a window. What room is that?"

"It's part of the gallery," Jillian said. "It's a portrait gallery full of paintings of people we don't really remember, which is a little sad when you think about it. And my family has been storing old junk up there for generations."

"Maybe something is close to the window and making the reflection on the glass wonky," Annika suggested. "At any rate, it's not broken."

"You're right."

They walked on to the backyard and again Jillian saw no sign of any broken windows. The garage addition blocked them from easily reaching the other side yard from the backyard, but they walked around the long addition, checking the second floor windows carefully. They turned the corner at the end and Annika pointed up. "Bingo!"

Jillian's gaze followed the direction the young actress was pointing. Sure enough, one of the windows on the second floor was broken. "That's one of the windows of the apartment bedroom."

"You have a whole apartment up there, and I had to share with Gloria?"

"Sorry about that." Jillian checked the ground for glass. If the bird flew into the window, it would have broken inward, so she shouldn't find the ground covered with glass. And she didn't. "I'll need to go upstairs and check on the apartment."

"Cool," Annika said. "I didn't get to see that part of the house."

"It's not that exciting. This is the newest part of the mansion. When the original part was built, before the Civil War, none of this back extension existed." She dug in her pants for the key and opened the door leading to the big garage. A steep flight of stairs at one end led up to the apartment.

"I wonder what was here back then," Annika said.

"I don't know. I'm not really that good at family history. Aunt Cornelia is probably the best, though I have to consider the possibility that she makes up stuff."

Annika laughed. "I have an uncle like that. According to him, our ancestors were made up of world-famous circus acrobats, Vikings, a vampire, and a smattering of royalty."

"A vampire?"

"That's a recent addition to the family-history stories," Annika said, "but I like it."

"I would recommend we introduce him to Cornelia, but that would probably be catastrophic."

They walked through the apartment quickly to reach the back bedroom. Luckily, there had been no bad weather since the window was broken, so the pretty carved-leg table under the window appeared to be undamaged, though it glittered with shards of glass. Jillian also noticed the room had more than the usual number of bugs. "I'll need to get this fixed before we get rain, and come back here with a flyswatter. Until then, I should find something to cover the window before we end up with bats in the house."

"Bats are cool," Annika said. "Except for the whole rabies thing. You know, if Kane gets out of the hospital soon, he could fix it for you. He's really handy. He worked with his uncle building houses."

Jillian was glad to hear Annika sounding more optimistic. Kane had looked so bad the night before, however, that she wasn't sure that optimism was warranted. They'd learned Kane was alive and conscious, but that didn't mean he was well. A knot of worry tightened in her belly. If Kane was attacked for finding this broken window, she couldn't think of a reason for it. The location certainly didn't leave her with any other clues. None of the crew should have been in this part of the house, so she couldn't imagine who might have found the crow after it broke the window, if indeed that was what had happened.

Annika bent down and picked up a fluffy black feather and held it out to Jillian. "I guess we know the crow got in this way."

Jillian took the feather and looked at it closely. She didn't know much about feathers, but it didn't look like the feathers she remembered on the dead bird.

Annika ran her hand over the rich golden wood of the tabletop. "At least the table wasn't damaged by all this glass."

That drew Jillian's attention away from the feather. She knelt closer to look at the table. "Actually there's a dent in the wood that I don't remember being there. The one thing I don't see is blood. How does a crow hurt itself that badly without leaving any blood on the broken glass or on this table that it apparently hit hard enough to dent?"

"That is weird," Annika said. "Maybe it didn't bleed right away. Maybe it flapped around and that opened the wound enough to bleed."

"Then we'd see blood on the floor somewhere," Jillian said. "Do you see any blood?"

Annika shook her head. "It could have done the flapping under the bed or something."

Jillian knelt and lifted the bedspread to look under the bed. She didn't find any blood, but she did find a smooth river rock, about the size of a baseball. It looked like one of the rocks Cornelia used to edge some of the flower beds.

She stood and held it up. "This rock wasn't in here earlier either, but it looks about the right size to make the dent in the table."

"Someone threw a rock through the window?" Annika said. "Why?"

Jillian studied the rock in her hand. "I wish I knew."

Jillian's head was whirling as she and Annika left the garage. The more information she gathered, the less it made sense. *Why would someone throw a rock through the apartment window?* It seemed pointless. Did the broken window have anything to do with Kane's injury? If the window wasn't broken by the bird, how did a black feather end up in the apartment? And if the bird didn't break the window, how did it end up dead on the floor of Gloria Baxter's bathroom? *Lots of questions, but not many answers.*

They walked along the side of the garage toward the porte cochere, and Annika kept looking upward. "You know, now that I know this back part is an addition, I can tell. Everything looks a little bit different on the new part."

Jillian looked at the last side of the house and the addition together. She stared up at them for a while. "It's the newer materials. No matter how much they try to make them match, they just don't."

"It's not really noticeable if you don't look too closely," the young actress said.

"No, overall they did a good job." Jillian finally gave up on fretting about the broken window. *Maybe if I do something else, my subconscious will sort through the pieces of this crazy puzzle.* "Let's see if we can find some cardboard to cover that broken window, and then we can finally finish the kitchen. At the rate I'm going it'll still be a mess when Bertie gets home."

"I imagine you'd hear about that."

"You know it."

Jillian stopped in the laundry room and grabbed one of the old yard-sale signs they kept stored behind the drying rack and a role of duct tape. The laminated sign would make a good temporary patch for the window. "I'm going to run back to the apartment and tape this over the window."

"I'll get started on the kitchen," Annika said, "and enjoy the air-conditioning."

"Thanks so much for your help."

Annika waved that off. "It gives me something to do. I've never done well when I have time and worry on my hands." She gave Jillian a mischievous smile. "It encourages me to look for trouble."

"We've had enough of that around here."

As Jillian headed back outside, the smack of humidity and heat made her understand Annika's decision. Jillian pinched the fabric of her light blouse and flapped it, letting the tiny breeze cool her sweaty skin. *I'll be glad when fall gets here.*

"Miss Green." The harsh whisper startled Jillian and she looked around for the speaker. "Jillian!" With the second call, Jillian was able to better pinpoint the direction, and she saw Bibi Bleu peeking around the corner of the garage. "Over here." The woman made a hurried beckoning gesture.

For a moment, Jillian debated the wisdom of approaching Gloria's assistant on her own. After all, Bibi might be the one responsible for two people in the hospital, but Jillian simply couldn't imagine the nervous woman attacking someone as big as Kane. Finally, her curiosity overrode common sense and she walked to the edge of the garage. "We've been worried about you," she said quietly.

Bibi reached out and snatched Jillian's arm, pulling her closer to the building. "I was hiding."

"Hiding? Where? Why?"

Bibi let go of Jillian's arm and made a vague gesture toward the back of the property. "I found a big building back there. There are mice, but it's actually not so bad. All the shade makes it cooler."

Jillian assumed Bibi was talking about their old tobacco barn. It was nice to know it had made such nice guest accommodations, but that didn't help her understand the situation. "Why are you hiding in our barn?"

"I don't want to end up like Gloria."

"Like Gloria? So you don't believe what happened to your boss was an accident? Or should I say, two accidents?"

Bibi shook her head. "I thought the fall was," she whispered hoarsely. "But I know someone tried to kill her at the hospital. I was in the bathroom. I heard!"

Jillian remembered Collette Rawles saying someone was in the bathroom. Apparently that someone was Bibi. "Someone heard you in there." She wondered suddenly if the story Collette told was a lie. *Had she been at the hospital for more than a photo?*

Bibi's eyes widened, showing considerably bloodshot whites. "I knew it. I knew I was heard." She put her hand to her mouth. "I'm going to die."

"No you're not," Jillian said, doing her best to imitate Bertie's no-nonsense tone. "You're going to tell the deputy what you heard and help get all this settled." Jillian pulled her phone from her pocket. "What did you hear?"

Bibi swatted at the phone in Jillian's hand. "Don't do that. The only reason I'm still alive is because the killer doesn't know I heard. If I tell the deputy, I'm as good as dead."

"Don't be ridiculous," Jillian snapped. "This is the real world, not some overwrought crime drama. Once you tell the deputy, he'll arrest the person and all of this will be over. We can stop looking over our shoulders."

Bibi shook her head over and over. "He'll kill me."

Jillian's attention snapped at the masculine pronoun. *Great. You eliminated my primary suspect right there.* "If you didn't come to tell what you know, why are you here?"

"I need to get out of here, but I don't have any money," Bibi said. "Gloria doesn't pay very well, and I don't have enough in the bank for a bus ticket home. The car I've been driving belongs to Gloria. If I took it, she'd have me arrested for grand theft auto."

"So you came back to the house to borrow money?" Jillian asked, spacing out each word in her astonishment. Did this stranger think Jillian was going to give her money? Judging by the look of relief that flooded Bibi's face, Bibi thought exactly that.

"I came back to hide. I figured there must be lots of places on the property to hide, and I was right, but I can't stay back there forever. I want to go home. I only need enough for a bus ticket," Bibi said. "And I'll pay you back someday. You must have the money, living in a big, beautiful house like this."

"You're laboring under a misconception," Jillian said. "The house belongs to my grandmother, and we're struggling to keep body and soul together here. Honestly, our income stream is a *bakery*. What made you think we were rich?"

Bibi began to wring her hands, her face a portrait of misery. "I don't know. I don't know. I don't know." She hiccupped as her eyes filled with tears. "You were so nice to me, and I'm desperate. I don't want to die."

"You're not going to die. Look, tell me what you heard, and we'll figure out what exactly to do about it. How's that?"

"I guess," Bibi whispered, snuffling.

"Then come on inside. I'll get you some nice cold tea, and you can have a shower and change your clothes."

Bibi's eyes sprang open wide again. "I can't go in there. He'll see me!"

Jillian looked at Bibi in surprise. "The person you heard is in the house?"

"Of course."

"Tell me," Jillian said. "Tell me right now."

Jillian's fierce tone must have alarmed the nervous woman because Bibi took a quick step back from Jillian. As it turned out, it was a good thing she did. At that exact moment, Jillian heard the distinct sound of gunshot as a bullet buried itself in the garage wall right between Jillian and Bibi.

As Jillian dove for the ground, she had one clear thought: *Why do people keep shooting at me?*

19

By the time Jillian was sure no more gunshots were following, she scrambled to her feet and saw that Bibi was long gone. She didn't want to be a target either, but where would she be truly safe? She looked back toward the house and shuddered as she pulled out her phone to call the police. *Was Bibi right? Has the person who attempted murder more than once been staying here the whole time?*

She walked under the porte cochere as she punched the buttons to call the police station directly. It wasn't that she didn't consider the shooting an emergency, but she thought it best to talk to Gooder directly and tell him what she knew so he'd be prepared when he arrived.

"Nathan County Sheriff's Department." The slightly nasal voice on the other end of the phone was immediately recognizable. It was Gooder's mother.

"Mrs. Jones, this is Jillian Green. There's been a shooting out here at Belle Haven."

"Who did you get shot this time?" the woman demanded.

I've never gotten anyone shot! "May I speak to your son? I believe this is Gooder's case."

"I'll transfer the call," the woman said grudgingly.

While Jillian waited, she thought of the black feather lying in the garage apartment, a feather that hadn't looked like a crow feather to her. Then the realization hit her. She knew exactly what kind of feather she'd found: It was a feather from Christopher Dark's ragged black leather vest. He'd stopped wearing the vest, but she remembered seeing a stray feather in the director's hair that was exactly the same kind of broad, fluffy feather that lay on the apartment floor.

Was Christopher Dark the one who'd put two people in the hospital? If so, why? Surely it didn't do him any good to have his movie fall apart. She shook off her uneasy musings as Gooder's voice came on the line. "You had a shooting?"

"Someone shot at either me or Bibi Bleu. No one was hit."

"Bibi Bleu? You found her?"

"She found me," Jillian said, "and then someone shot at us. I'm thinking the shooting part is really the important part here. Bibi said she overheard the person who came to kill Gloria in the hospital. She knows who it is, but she wouldn't tell me. It's someone staying here at the house."

"Of course it is," Gooder said. "You attract the most interesting people, Jillian. I'll be right out." Then he hung up before Jillian could comment on his remark. *At least he didn't blame the shooting on hunters like he did the first time someone tried to shoot me.*

She walked into the house and found Annika busily wiping the kitchen counters, earbuds blasting music with enough volume that Jillian could pick out the song. *No wonder she didn't come out to check on the gunshot.* Then Jillian had a chilling thought. *Why didn't Cornelia come out and check?*

"I'm almost done," Annika said, removing an earbud. "Did you get the window patched?"

"Actually I was distracted. Did anyone come through here? Maybe Christopher?"

"I haven't seen anyone," Annika said.

"I need to check on Aunt Cornelia," Jillian said. "I'll be right back."

"No problem." Annika shoved the earbud back in her ear and carried her dishcloth over to the sink.

Jillian practically sprinted into the living room, where she found Cornelia sitting in one of the cozy chairs, a book in her lap and her head tilted forward on her chest. For an instant, Jillian had the terrifying thought that her aunt might be dead. She crossed the room quickly and heard Cornelia's soft snoring.

She reached out and gently shook the older woman awake. "Jillian?" Cornelia said. "What's the matter, dear?"

"Deputy Jones is on his way over," Jillian said. She quickly explained about what had happened outside. "When he gets here, can you lead him back to the tobacco barn? If Bibi ran back there, I want to make sure she's okay."

Cornelia nodded hesitantly. "Maybe you should wait until the deputy gets here."

Jillian shook her head, dropping her voice to a whisper. "If Christopher followed Bibi back there, she may need my help."

"Christopher?" Cornelia sat up even straighter. "What does he have to do with anything?"

"I think he's the one behind this." She explained about the broken window and the feather.

"All the more reason to wait until Gooder gets here."

"I can't. You wait for Gooder, and stay away from Christopher Dark."

Before Jillian could leave, Cornelia grabbed her hand. "Find Leo. Take him with you. He'll make Christopher think twice about doing anything."

"Christopher attacked Kane," Jillian said. "He's not going to be afraid of Leo. Besides, Leo isn't here. He went to the hotel to tell the rest of the crew the good news about Gloria and Kane."

"Wait for Gooder," Cornelia said. "Please. This is exactly the kind of behavior in horror movies that gets people killed."

"This isn't a movie. I'll be careful, but I need to get Bibi somewhere safe. Send Gooder to the tobacco barn. He'll be here soon."

Cornelia stood and followed Jillian to French doors that led from the living room to the back porch, "The tear-out cards said this would be solved by a healthy police officer. That might be Gooder," she said, her voice full of hope. "Just don't get shot before he gets here."

Jillian squeezed her aunt's hand. "That's the plan."

She slipped outside and headed to the right, planning to approach the backyard from the far right so that the shadows of the trees would give her cover. If Christopher had gone inside instead of following Bibi, she didn't want him to catch sight of her. As she reached the tree line, she paused for a moment, listening for the sound of sirens or any cars on the drive. The yard was silent except for the drone of buzzing insects and the desultory chirping of birds, apparently feeling no livelier in the heat than the humans.

Jillian moved through the thick brush at the back of the yard as quietly as she could, not wanting to alert Christopher if he was out there with a gun. Jillian hoped the loud drone of the insects would drown out any small twig snaps or the rustle of her passage through the woods.

Jillian hadn't been inside the tobacco barn where Bibi had been staying in years. She'd intended to check it out, but it was just one more thing on her list she hadn't gotten to yet. The location wasn't too far from the house, and it could be a possible event venue if the structure was sound enough to renovate. Of course, there was a lot of brush between the house and the barn that would have to be removed, and that wouldn't be cheap.

What am I doing thinking about money when there's someone with a gun out here? She gave herself a mental shake, sharpening her focus that was dulled by the heat and droning buzz. This was no time to be distracted.

As she approached the tobacco barn, Jillian thought it looked a lot better than she expected. No wonder Bibi had taken refuge there. The walls seemed to be sound, at least as far as Jillian could see. The barn was long and narrow, but tall to allow for plenty of beams for hanging tobacco to dry. It had no windows, but the door was missing, looking like a dark hole that no sensible person would enter.

Jillian took a deep breath and stepped silently into the darkness. She listened carefully for any sound inside the barn that might indicate someone moving around. She heard nothing. The barn smelled of wet wood with a trace of very old tobacco scent. "Bibi?" Jillian whispered. "Bibi, are you here?"

She stepped deeper into the darkness, wishing desperately that she'd thought to bring a flashlight. Her eyes were slowly adjusting to the dim light, but she could see little beyond her immediate location. Then a hand darted out of the darkness and caught hold of her sweat-slippery hand, making Jillian yelp.

"Shh," Bibi scolded in a fierce whisper. "He'll hear you."

"Is Christopher here?" Jillian whispered back.

"I don't know," Bibi said. "Did he come with you?"

"Of course not. I wouldn't intentionally lead him out here to you. I called the sheriff's office. Deputy Jones is on the way. It's going to be okay. He'll arrest Christopher."

Though Jillian could barely make out the other woman's face, her tone was full of confusion. "Why would he arrest Christopher?"

"For trying to kill Gloria and Kane."

Jillian heard a sharp intake of breath. "Someone tried to kill Kane? Why? He's so sweet."

"I don't know," Jillian said. "But I also don't know why Christopher tried to kill Gloria."

"Christopher didn't try to kill Gloria," Bibi said.

"What?"

"Christopher didn't try to kill Gloria. I mean, I suppose he could be the one who pushed her down. She never would tell me who did that, but he's not the person who came into the hospital room and gave her the injection."

"But I found one of the feathers from his vest in the garage apartment."

"I have no idea what you're talking about," Bibi's soft whisper grew louder as she clearly became frustrated with Jillian.

"Fine, then who did try to kill Gloria?"

"I'm afraid that would be me."

Jillian and Bibi both turned sharply back toward the doorway to the big barn. The man standing in the doorway looked even taller and far more imposing than Jillian remembered. Shock made her slow to process what she was seeing. Finally she managed to croak, "Leo?"

20

"Yes ma'am," the tall actor said, nodding slightly in Jillian's direction. "I'm real sorry that you and Bibi and Kane got tangled up in this."

"I don't understand," Jillian said. "Why are you doing this?"

"I had to," Leo said, taking several steps closer to them. He was still backlit from the doorway, and Jillian couldn't see his face. "She had to pay."

"Pay for what?" Jillian asked, taking a careful step in front of Bibi. If she was putting herself in danger for the other woman, she was going to commit to it. If she kept Leo talking, maybe Bibi could slip away into the darkness. Jillian tried to remember if the old barn had more than one door, but she suspected it didn't. "What could an old woman possibly have done?"

"She killed my sister."

"Your sister?"

"Annie Venture was my sister," Leo said. "She was a few years older than me, but I went into acting as a way of honoring her after her tragic accident. Of course, it wasn't an accident at all."

"You think Gloria stabbed your sister with a knife on purpose?"

He nodded. "I met a man who'd worked on *Hexe*. He said he was sure Gloria had killed my sister on purpose to get her role. I wasn't convinced, so I pushed my agent to get me on this film. Then once I met Gloria, I could see it. I could see guilt all over her."

"Why is your name Shone and not Venture?" Jillian asked. Gooder had to be along soon, *surely*. If she could keep Leo talking until Gooder got there, they might all be okay.

"Our name was Shubbens," Leo said. "No one kept their real name back then." He took another step toward Jillian. "I'm sorry, but I can't let you or Bibi tell anyone what you know." He raised his hand and Jillian saw the dark outline of a handgun.

"Are you threatening my granddaughter, Leo Shone?" Bertie's voice cut through the darkness like a knife. Jillian actually had to lean to see around Leo to her grandmother in the doorway. Bertie and Cornelia stood together in the light of the doorway. Cornelia held a heavy walking stick that normally stood in a fancy bucket in the library, and Bertie carried a shotgun that looked nearly as old as the tobacco barn they stood in. The shotgun was trained on Leo.

Jillian looked wide-eyed at her grandmother. Knowing the spray of those old shotguns, there was every chance that she could end up shot as well. "I'm sure Leo will put down the gun now."

"Bertie," Leo said softly, "I had to do something. Gloria killed my sister."

"Maybe," Bertie snapped. "Maybe not. But Kane didn't kill your sister and neither did Bibi or my granddaughter. You have a lot to answer for Leo Shone, and you're going to answer for it, or I'll shoot you where you stand."

"You wouldn't," Leo said softly.

"To protect my granddaughter, I'd do just about anything," Bertie said.

"Me too," Cornelia added, and with a dramatic flourish, she twisted the end of the walking stick and pulled out a long, thin sword.

Leo seemed to visibly wilt in the face of the two old ladies. Apparently his willingness to hurt people to cover up his crimes had a limit. Jillian slipped up and took the gun out of his hand.

A bellow came from the dense brush between the barn and

the house. "Jillian!" She recognized the voice of Deputy Jones. "Where are you? You'd better not be dead. The paperwork is terrible if you got yourself dead."

"That's Gooder," Jillian said. "Always the humanitarian."

"Why did Leo knock Kane on the head?"

The question came from Hunter, who had listened avidly to Jillian's story of all the events that happened since he'd seen Jillian last. He'd waved the waiter away twice so that the tale wouldn't be interrupted. Jillian appreciated his enthusiasm, but she really did want a piece of apple pie. "Apparently Kane noticed what I noticed. One of the windows to the third-floor gallery looked funny. Only Kane knew what it meant because he'd seen old window glass when he worked construction. Someone had replaced the old glass with new. That window is the one the crow flew into."

Hunter took a sip of his iced tea, as she spoke. "So the bird really did die of natural causes, sort of. But that doesn't explain the second broken window or the feather you found."

"Leo broke the window with a rock and left the feather to draw attention to Christopher. His vest was shedding feathers every time he wore it, but they were dyed turkey feathers, not crow."

He blinked as he absorbed that. "Then Leo found the dead crow and moved it?"

"Yeah. Apparently Leo heard it break through the gallery window and thought it would be a great symbol for Gloria since he thought she was a murderer."

"Was she?"

"Apparently not. It was just some wild theory from a guy who'd been nursing a grudge against Gloria for years. Thankfully, that grudge didn't result in anyone's death."

"That's true." Hunter smiled at her. "You liked him? Leo?"

"I did. And Bertie did too, though she'll never admit it. I think Leo liked us too. That's why he left so many notes, trying to warn me away so I wouldn't put myself in a position where he felt like he had to hurt me."

"But he seemed willing enough to hurt you and Bibi at the end."

Jillian nodded, the thought making her sad. She gazed around the room.

"I see you giving the waiter hopeful looks. You want dessert?"

"They have great pie here. Nearly as good as Bertie's."

"Then we should have some." Hunter held up a hand and the waiter rushed over to take their dessert order. After the waiter scurried off to retrieve the pie, Hunter turned back to the topic at hand. "So what happens with the movie?"

"Surprisingly, they'll be finishing it. Apparently all of Leo's scenes were done, and Cornelia will be taking over for Gloria, who is retiring from moviemaking. Now they're planning to have Cornelia voice-over the scenes shot by Gloria instead of the other way around. The doctors are pretty sure Gloria will recover fully from the drug Leo gave her, but she can't hide her other problem anymore."

"Other problem?"

"Dementia. She really was having trouble with her lines and wandering off. Her family has flown in, and they're taking her back to California. Gloria insisted Bibi remain with her as her assistant, though I expect they'll need a nurse too."

"And Kane?"

"He gets headaches if he's out in the heat too long, but the doctors have cleared him to finish. And he and Annika have decided not to hide their relationship anymore, which hasn't brought more paparazzi to Belle Haven . . . yet."

"You can always sic Cornelia and her cane on them if they show up."

Jillian groaned. "Cornelia is convinced now that her tear-out cards predicted a male actor as the culprit." She explained about the magazine-card prophesy and Hunter laughed. "She says she just needs to learn to read them better."

"Maybe she'll focus on acting for a while," he said.

"We can hope. At any rate, Christopher is thrilled to have the chance to finish the movie, and I'm glad that The Chocolate Shoppe Bakery will be getting paid in full for our work."

"So it sounds like a happy ending." Hunter took another sip of his tea, then added, "Except for one thing."

"What's that?"

"You definitely did not do as I asked. You weren't careful. You weren't even a little bit careful."

Jillian held up her hand. "Bertie already read me the riot act—repeatedly, I assure you. I am so chastised."

Hunter smiled at her. "But you'll do it again. Running into danger is far too much a part of all you Belle Haven women."

Jillian shrugged. "Maybe."

"Then I guess I'll have to get used to it," he said, "or stick a little closer to keep you safe."

This time it was Jillian's turn to smile. "I would probably be all right with that."

Scone Cold Revenge
Book Five Recipe

Chocolate Orange Scones

Scones

½ cup butter
1⅔ cup flour
⅓ cup cocoa powder
½ cup sugar
2½ teaspoons baking powder
¾ teaspoon cinnamon

Zest of 1 orange
½ teaspoon salt
½ cup heavy cream
1 large egg
1½ teaspoons vanilla

Icing

1 chocolate bar
Juice of 1 orange

Confectioners' sugar

Instructions

Preheat oven to 400 degrees.

1. Adjust oven rack to middle-low position.

2. Cut butter into very small cubes and stash in freezer.

3. In a large bowl, whisk together flour, cocoa, sugar, baking powder, cinnamon, orange zest, and salt until thoroughly mixed.

4 Chop up frozen butter cubes. (If they begin to soften from the chop, chill for a few minutes before going on to the next step.) Cut in chopped, frozen butter with pastry cutter or two table knives until the mixture resembles coarse meal. Set aside.

5. In a small bowl, thoroughly whisk together cream, egg, and vanilla. Pour slowly into flour mixture, a little at a time, tossing mixture with flexible spatula with each addition until everything is moistened and mixture comes together into dough. (More heavy cream may be added a teaspoon at a time if needed.) Don't overwork the dough.

6. Flour hands and transfer dough ball to parchment-lined baking sheet. Press out into an 8-inch disk. Cut disk into 8 wedges with large lightly floured pizza cutter or large knife. Separate wedges on baking sheet.

7. Bake for 20 minutes. Remove scones and allow to cool slightly while you make icing.

8. For icing: break chocolate bar into small pieces and place in microwave safe bowl. Microwave in 15-second intervals, stirring after each interval, until chocolate is melted and smooth. Add orange juice. Then sift in confectioners' sugar, stirring rapidly until icing is thickened. Drizzle over warm scones. Serve immediately or allow to cool completely and store in airtight container.

Yield: 8 scones